'Blindness hasn't deprived me of all my strength or ability.'

'I never for one moment supposed that it had,' replied Emma primly, massaging her sore wrist and privately thinking how strong the professor was. 'You're the only one who keeps harping on about your disability, not me. We're only too anxious to see you as you were, or as you might be if you stopped feeling so bloody sorry for yourself.'

There was a long silence, heavy with undigested thoughts and unspoken words.

'Well, Emma Seymour, there is certainly more to you than just a pretty face, which my brother has described to me, or a pretty voice, which I can assess for myself. Shall we call it a truce, Miss Seymour?' James asked.

Margaret O'Neill started scribbling at four and began nursing at twenty. She contracted TB, and, when recovered, did her British Tuberculosis Association nursing training before general training at the Royal Portsmouth Hospital. She married, had two children, and with her late husband she owned and managed several nursing homes. Now retired and living in Sussex, she still has many nursing contacts. Her husband would have been delighted to see her books in print.

Previous titles

A QUESTION OF HONOUR
COTTAGE HOSPITAL

# DOCTOR
# ON SKYE

BY

MARGARET O'NEILL

**MILLS & BOON LIMITED**
ETON HOUSE   18–24 PARADISE ROAD
RICHMOND   SURREY   TW9 1SR

*First published in Great Britain 1992
by Mills & Boon Limited*

© Margaret O'Neill 1992

*Australian copyright 1992
Philippine copyright 1992
This edition 1992*

ISBN 0 263 77592 5

Set in 10 on 12 pt Linotron Times
03-9203-53051
*Typeset in Great Britain by Centracet, Cambridge
Made and printed in Great Britain*

# CHAPTER ONE

By a mixture of transport—train, road, air and sea—she had arrived.

'I'm Emma Seymour,' she said, advancing to meet the man before her, and speaking as she went so that he would be aware of her position in the room. She put her outstretched hand firmly into his, remembering that the matron at St Dunstan's, where they specialised in caring for the blind, had instructed, 'Be positive; let the patient feel that you are there. Give that person a chance to respond once he or she has felt your hand.'

Professor James MacDonald gripped her hand as firmly as she held his, and gave her a smile that could only be described as wry. Composed of a lop-sided quirked-up lip and raised eyebrows, it plainly proclaimed, as if in words, Don't play that textbook game with me; I'm made of sterner stuff.

His conventional reply, though, was as might have been expected.

'Nice of you to come, Miss Seymour, I do hope that you had a good journey.' His voice was deep, rather gravelly.

'Oh, it was marvellous, thanks to the meticulous arrangements that you made for me.'

The professor threw back his head and gave a great guffaw of laughter.

'I made! My dear girl, I haven't made arrangements for anyone to do anything for months.' His voice sounded harsh. 'I haven't done anything of value for months, not even arrange an itinerary that any idiot could organise.'

Emma thought that she had never heard anything said so bitterly before. She was determined not to be disconcerted by the venomous tone, and sought for some neat, sensible reply. Before she could open her mouth, Dr Angus MacDonald, the professor's younger brother and her escort from Inverness, spoke for her.

'That's a bloody awful way to speak to a visitor, James. I think you owe Emma—er—Miss Seymour an apology.'

The professor's handsome face, half concealed though it was by the dark glasses covering both eyes, betrayed continuing anger. His lips were tightly compressed, nostrils of a splendid high-bridged nose flaring and a determined chin jutting mutinously. The deeply scored lines associated with pain and fatigue, round his mouth and down lean cheeks, seemed to deepen as he drew in a frustrated breath and turned his head slightly in his brother's direction. He ran a thin brown hand through his mop of wiry hair, jet-black except where a snow-white streak lacerated it from temple to nape.

'Angus, playing the knight errant already!' The professor's voice was heavy with sarcasm. 'I'm sure Miss Seymour or—er—Emma, being the outright winner over many young women for the dubious privilege of acting as my secretary cum nurse, is more than able to put up with my rudeness. I doubt that she needs you to ride shotgun.'

Emma realised that he was winding her up because of his hatred and resentment at being blind and dependent. But she couldn't let him get away entirely with being so bad-mannered, a trait that she wouldn't think he normally subscribed to. She must set some working boundaries right from the start.

'You're quite right, Professor, my proven ability to withstand a few slings and arrows was one of the attributes that put me ahead of my competitors. I don't doubt that others were as well or better qualified in other respects.'

The professor's mouth lifted at the corners, both corners this time, Emma noted, and he gave a soft chuckle.

'Ah, yes, a particularly unpleasant, dictatorial aunt who succeeded in interrupting your career, breaking up your engagement and virtually leaving you homeless. It's all here, a complete dossier, you might say, setting out your reasons for being suitable to act as my keeper-secretary.' He turned his head in his brother's direction. 'There we are, Angus, no male chauvinistic support required. Miss—or should I say Ms?—Emma Seymour needs you not and is determined to keep her patient in order.'

Dr MacDonald made an impatient snorting sound and spread out his hands in an eloquent gesture of despair.

'I must apologise for my brother, Emma.' He gave her a lop-sided grin, rather like the professor's but without the cynicism. 'He was always a caustic beggar, but regretfully his present indisposition has made him downright rude.'

Emma gave him such a warm smile that he almost physically rocked on his heels. Suddenly he was even more acutely aware of her beauty than at their first encounter. He stared at her hard, meeting her green eyes with his of slaty blue, admiring her thick silver-fair hair, cut into a bob, with a fringe falling almost to meet dark, straight smudges of eyebrows. He took in, too, the tipped-up nose, wide, generous mouth and dimpled cheeks. For a moment he was both glad and sorry that James couldn't see and appreciate this lovely girl.

Glad, because if he saw, and chose to, he would no doubt conquer as he always had every attractive female within his ken. Sorry, because his much-loved brother was bereft of sight, which, together with his trained and nimble fingers and fine intelligence, was his most valuable asset.

She said, in answer to the professor's sarcastic query about how to address her, 'I think that Emma would do very nicely, or Miss Seymour, if you prefer, Professor.'

He suddenly seemed to tire of the game of crossing swords with his new employee and rapped out sharply, 'Emma, sensible, no-nonsense Emma, so be it.' He turned his head away from her and stretched out a hand to an old-fashioned bell-pull by the huge fireplace, filled at the moment with an urn full of spiky delphiniums and foxgloves. 'I'm sure you'll want to see your room and get settled in. Coffee, say, in twenty minutes?'

A rotund, cheerful little lady appeared in answer to the bell-pull.

'You rang, Professor?' she asked in a soft Highland accent.

'Aye, Mrs Mac. This is our visitor, Miss Seymour. Emma, let me introduce Mrs Mac, who looks after us all and has done for as long as I can remember.'

Emma stretched out a hand and had it warmly clasped by one that was plump and rough.

The same soft voice bade her welcome and smiled in

a homely, motherly way that seemed to endorse her words.

'Come along with me, Miss Seymour, and see if your room's to your liking. Now you're to be telling me if there's aught else that you need.'

The stout little body led her from the room and up a magnificent staircase that glowed with a golden sheen achieved by years of polishing.

'Chestnut,' said Mrs Mac, seeing Emma stroke the wooden banister as they ascended the stairs. 'Brought over by the Laird MacDonald when he built the house here at the turn of the century.'

There was a wide landing at the top of the staircase opening to the left and right. From this two smaller staircases at either end rose to a second storey. Opposite each staircase a narrower, though still generous, corridor opened up to reveal more rooms at the back of the house. It was down the right-hand one of these that Mrs Mac led Emma.

She flung open the second door along the corridor and invited her to enter.

It was difficult to take in at first. Such elegance, combined with comfort and homeliness. A white, bright room lit by a huge picture-window looking out over a garden which sloped upwards to fields beyond, where long-horned Highland cattle grazed. A carpet of some soft oatmeal colour covered the bedroom and the adjacent bathroom floors. The woodwork was off-white, the walls faintly pink and hung with paintings. Most were of country scenes, soft, unobtrusive, muted greens and browns, but these were interspersed by a vivid splash of red poppies on one wall and an equally vibrant orange and lemon stylised picture of nasturtiums in full bloom on another.

Seeing her interest, Mrs Mac explained, 'Jamie did
those years ago when he was recovering from flu as a
wee laddie of sixteen. "Let's cheer ourselves and the
natives up, Mrs Mac," I remember him saying. Aye,
he was a bonny brave lad who steered us through that
long grey winter. The laird had just died of the same
flu that struck him, and Mistress MacDonald was
grieving and greeting her own life away.' The housekeeper gave Emma a watery smile and smoothed down
her apron. 'But there, lass, ye won't be wanting to hear
all our past problems—we've enough to be going on
with at the present time with the professor losing the
sight of his eyes and being so poorly.'

'My goodness, he's very talented. Does he still
paint?' Even as she asked, Emma realised how silly it
was. How could the poor man paint, blind as he was,
even if, hopefully, temporarily?

Mrs Mac seemed not to notice the ambiguity of the
question.

'Aye, lass, of course he does. It's his outlet, his way
of relaxing. He's had an exhibition, ye ken, in
Edinburgh the year before last. Sold everything, he
did. Has it from Mistress MacDonald, the flair for
putting paint on paper. She was a great one for the
water-colours, was the mistress.'

A few minutes later, after Mrs Mac had left and she
had tided herself in the sumptuously equipped bathroom, Emma sat down to think before returning to the
sitting-room and the brothers MacDonald.

Her mind was in tumult. There was so much to take
in. The soft, drawling Highland accent of Mrs Mac and
the other locals she had spoken to on her journey. The
less obvious accents of the professor and his brother;
just a faint burr overlaid by conventional educated

English. The professor's antagonism and resentment, which she understood and hoped she could cope with.

She thought about the advertisement that had stimulated her to apply for the post of secretary-nurse to Professor James MacDonald. It had been uncompromising, straight to the point. No fancy language about paragons of virtue or Girl Fridays being required, to hide the fact that there was a difficult post to fill.

The wording of the advertisement in the *Nursing Times* and *The Lady* was indelibly printed on her mind, mainly because she had answered it in a moment of despondency and without hope of being considered, or even minding much if she was or not.

WANTED for a minimum two-month contract, a RGN with secretarial skills. Knowledge of word processor an advantage. Successful applicant to work in Isle of Skye for professional, temporarily unsighted person. Unsocial hours to be expected, reflected in generous salary. Minimal nursing but skilled duties required. Ophthalmic nursing useful and patient care on a one-to-one basis. CV written and on tape, and other relevant information to: Professor James MacDonald, The Old House, by Tarskaveig Bay, Sleat, Isle of Skye.

Her CV, and, as she had later learned, particularly her voice tape, had procured her an interview in London with the professor's sister, Dr Philippa MacDonald. She was a registrar at Charing Cross, a busy person fitting in the onerous task of interviewing applicants on her brother's behalf with difficulty. It had been quite obvious, though, that she held the professor in great esteem and affection and was determined to find for him the right person to fit his requirements.

'Most of all,' she had told Emma, 'my brother liked
your voice. Melodious, he called it, and, since he will
have to listen to it with the acute hearing of the blind
that he's acquired recently, it's a very important factor.'
She had grinned widely, a nice, friendly smile that
Emma had responded to, and continued, 'We've had
so many well-qualified people apply for the job. I
didn't realise how many nurses were also efficient in
secretarial skills. But only a few suited James voice-
wise. Yourself and three other women from here in the
south, and a recently qualified Scottish nurse, who is
being interviewed in Edinburgh by my brother Angus.'

'What happens now?' Emma had asked at the end of
the interview. 'Will you or your brother get in touch?'

'Certainly, and, if I have anything to do with it, you
will be successful.' Dr MacDonald had looked a little
uncomfortable. 'Oh, dear, perhaps I shouldn't have
said that, but, as I've interviewed the others here,
you're the person I shall be recommending to James.'

'So it's between me and the Scottish nurse?'

'Yes, so it would seem.'

Emma had written off her chances of getting the
post. After all, it was surely more likely that a
Scotswoman with equal qualifications and presumably
a 'melodious' voice would land the job with a Scottish
professor of distinguished lineage.

A week had gone by, and then to her surprise she
received a phone call from Dr Philippa saying that she
had been chosen for the post.

'Can we meet at the same hotel the day after
tomorrow?' she had asked. 'To arrange about travelling
and dates, et cetera?'

'Of course. What time would suit you?'

They had agreed on a mutually suitable time. And

after that, reflected Emma, everything seemed to have been taken out of her hands.

The advertisement hadn't been kidding about the salary; it was very generous indeed. Dr Philippa, apparently at her brother James's insistence, had handed over a substantial sum against fares and overnight hotel accommodation. The time of journey and ways and means of travel had been arranged; nothing had been left to chance. A great relief after a year or more spent planning everything for a difficult and demanding patient, who also happened to be her aunt.

Emma had felt positively cosseted and cared for, and had had to remind herself that she would probably pay in kind for the trouble being taken. Surely no one, and especially a canny Scot, would throw money about so lavishly without good reason? Well, Dr Philippa MacDonald had been honest about her brother's being a difficult patient and a tough man to work for.

'He really doesn't suffer fools gladly,' she'd said, 'though he is the kindest and most considerate man in the world under normal circumstances.'

Having now met him, albeit briefly, Emma could well believe the first part of the description that his sister had given of him. She was not so sure about the second part; nothing in his manner had indicated kindness or consideration.

By the time she left her room within the twenty minutes stipulated by the professor all her nursing instincts as well as her kind and generous nature had come to her aid. The poor man had suffered enough, going partially blind through injury and, on top of that, falling foul of a severe infection. This had aggravated his eye condition, delayed his recovery and left him with post-viral fatigue. A fact, his sister had explained, he was reluctant to admit.

Emma decided as she descended the stairs that she would give him all the tender loving care of a nurse that he was entitled to. In addition, she would bear with his probable exacting demands in her secretarial capacity with patience and fortitude. She'd had plenty of practice exercising all these virtues over the period she'd cared for her ungrateful relation. At least here the surroundings were superb, her room delightful and some members of the household—in the shape of Mrs Mac and, while he was in residence, Angus MacDonald —friendly.

And who knows, she said to herself as she stepped from the stairs into the spacious entrance hall, lit by summer sunshine and fragrant with the scent of roses, perhaps the professor will turn out not to be such an ogre after all. She giggled to herself. Perhaps there's a mellow side to him that time will reveal.

She entered the sitting-room and joined the two brothers for coffee.

# CHAPTER TWO

IT TOOK several days to settle in. Emma loved her room with its tiny balcony opening from french windows looking out over the fabulous rose garden. Standing on the balcony and looking south, she could glimpse a corner of the bay, with a rocky outcrop sprouting a magnificent rowan tree and several small pines. The sandy, rocky beach looked golden in the early or evening sunlight, but was bleached to a colourless hue at midday. At night, under the full moon at present filling the few hours of darkness, it looked all silver.

Angus remained on Skye for two days after her arrival. She was grateful for his presence, and for the first time looked at him thoroughly. When he had met her at Inverness she had scarcely given him a glance or a thought, so anxious had she been to meet the professor. He was as different from his elder brother as it was possible to be, shorter than James's six feet plus by several inches, reddish-fair hair, where his brother was dark, his slaty blue eyes surveying her from a round, almost childish face, unlined, generally smiling. He was a happy, uncomplicated person, unlike his elder brother, who seemed to exist with a dark, romantic, Celtic aura around him, full of smouldering emotions held, with difficulty, in control.

The day after her arrival Emma had a long session with the professor in his study, a large book-lined room with panoramic views over the bay.

'Wasted on me,' said the professor as she entered to

15

find him sitting in a deep leather armchair. He waved his arm in the direction of the picture-window. His voice was as bitter as the day before.

'Not forever, Professor, unlike for some people. At least you have some sight in one eye and the chance of returning sight in the other.'

Her reply neither impressed nor comforted him.

'What the hell can I do in my line of work with eyes like these?' He jabbed a finger savagely at his dark spectacles.

'Don't!' cried Emma, hurrying forward and grabbing at his hand, afraid that he might damage himself. She caught his wrist and held it as tightly as possible.

He gave her a cruel, lop-sided grin like the one he had greeted her with on her arrival.

'I have only to twist my hand so,' he said in a nasty, smiling voice, 'to free it thus.' He suited action to words and slipped his hand free. 'Blindness hasn't deprived me of all my strength or ability,' he declared in a satisfied manner.

'I never for one moment supposed that it had,' replied Emma primly, massaging her sore wrist and privately thinking how strong he was. 'You're the only one who keeps harping on about your disability, not me, or any of the others here, or your sister in London. They are only too anxious to see you as you were, or as you might be if you stopped feeling so bloody sorry for yourself.'

She expected that he would be very angry indeed and order her out of the house. Fleetingly she thought that it was a good job that Angus was still around. He would be sympathetic in spite of his devotion to his brother, and fix her return journey without dispute.

There was a long silence, heavy with undigested

thoughts and unspoken words, while the professor sat, hands together, almost as if in prayer. When he spoke it was in a mild, soft Highland voice.

'Well, Emma Seymour, there is certainly more to you than just a pretty face, which my brother has described to me, or a pretty voice, which I can assess for myself.' He heaved himself out of the chair. 'Are you sitting at the other side of the desk?'

'No, I'm standing by the window, to the left of the grand piano.'

Every inch of her wanted to go towards him, meet him halfway; but some instinct born out of a mixture of her sensible nature and nursing training told her to stand still and let him come to her.

There were rich, silky rugs of glowing colours on the polished wood floor between them, and she was terrified that he would trip over them. He didn't. His memory, which she was later to discover was phenomenal, reminded him at every step of the hazards before him. He stepped over or round all obstacles, including a small coffee-table and an elegant Regency chair.

When he reached her he stretched out his right hand.

'Shall we call it a truce, Miss Seymour?' he asked. 'I'll try to be less evil-tempered, if you'll bear with my whims on a day-to-day basis.'

His voice was soft, gentle, pleading.

'I'm willing to give it a go, Professor, if you are.'

'So be it.'

They shook hands.

'Now,' he said abruptly, 'a little more information about my condition.' He seated himself in a cane chair in the window embrasure and indicated that she should do the same. 'Please sit down—I'm sorry, but I can't stand for too long; my ulcerated leg and the supreme effort of remembering where everything is drain one's energy.'

It was his first admission of inadequacy, and Emma was inclined to be magnanimous.

'You manage marvellously,' she said, hoping that she didn't sound too fulsome.

'Heaven forbid that you should praise me too much,' he said, a genuine laugh in his voice, then added very soberly, 'I look not for praise, but for help, and I think you might be brave enough, as well as trained enough, to give it.'

'I shall always do my best, Professor,' Emma answered, 'come hell or high water, and in spite of your bad temper.'

James MacDonald shouted with laughter.

'If anyone can set me on the road to recovery, Emma, you can,' he replied. 'Now, you know that I've been receiving treatment for my eyes since they were injured by the explosion.'

'Yes, your sister explained the situation to me at my interview in London.'

'And she presumably also explained that I had a subsequent infection that prevented immediate improvement to my eyes, and held up the healing of my damaged leg?'

'Yes.'

The brevity of her answer seemed at first to discon-cert him, but he quickly recovered.

'So you understand that I'm on irrigation treatment for both eyes until the suppuration ceases, and intra-muscular injections twice a day for infection, both general and particular.'

Again Emma thought it wiser, as well as accurate, simply to confirm what he had said.

'Yes.'

'I'm also having IMI of vitamins A, K, and C to supplement my food intake. Did you know that?'

'Yes.'

'Philippa seems to have filled you in pretty completely.'

'Did you expect her to do otherwise? She's a very competent doctor.'

'How do you know that?'

'I've nursing colleagues at Charing Cross who know her.'

'Of course, the medical and nursing world is a small one.'

'Yes.'

Suddenly, sardonically, he said, 'If you hadn't already proved otherwise, I would have taken it that you were simply a yes-woman.'

'I'm anything but, Professor,' said Emma. 'Don't be fooled by my agreeing with what you say. I'm not now or ever likely to say yes just to please you.'

Again he gave a great laugh that completely transformed his features, and she could imagine that even his eyes would be smiling at present, if they were able. It occurred to her then that she didn't know the colour of his eyes. Were they, she wondered, slaty blue like his brother's, or hazel brown like Philippa's? Well, she would soon know when she swabbed and irrigated them later, even though the corneas were damaged and the lids swollen.

'The ulcer on my leg,' the professor was saying as she mused about his eyes, 'is healing slowly, granulating at last. Even that has been slowed up because of the infection. Ridiculous—it wasn't a very large wound.'

'But deep, I understand.'

'Yes, bloody nuisance.' He banged the arms of the cane chair, which was obviously less fragile than it looked, since it withstood the attack without giving way. 'Anyway, enough of my ailments. Hector—Dr MacLeod, my GP and an old friend—will be in later to talk to you about dressings and things like that.'

He hadn't mentioned his myalgic encephalomyelitis, Emma noted, presumably because he didn't want to acknowledge that he was suffering from this fatigue syndrome. Strange how even educated and intelligent people could convince themselves that, by not speaking of something, it would go away. His sister had warned her of this, of course, and now, having met him, she could understand how a man of his strength and character must resent a condition so outside his control and only recently acknowledged medically to exist.

He said abruptly, as if reading her thoughts, 'You know about this ME thing, I suppose.'

'Yes, your sister spoke to me about it.'

'I suppose she also told you that I wouldn't accept that I'd got it because of pride and all that rubbish.'

'She said that you found it hard to come to terms with it.'

He snorted. 'Well, I did, but I have. And I can tell you, Emma, that it wasn't pride, just medical disbelief in a condition so impossible to pin down. But I met an old friend recently—he's here on holiday on the island. A distinguished physician. He accepts that it exists, knows someone with a similar history to mine who's been suffering from it for a year or so, but is now on the mend. He—Toby—is working out a treatment sheet for me, with Hector's consent, of course, and that of the consultant looking after my eyes.'

Emma was surprised at the amount of information he had chosen to give her. She had a feeling that he hadn't meant to confide more than was strictly necessary for her to carry out the simple nursing procedures required. And yet this last piece of information about the ME was more than she could have hoped for. It really looked as if he was going to trust her, at least on a professional level.

Somehow the knowledge made him seem very vulnerable, stripped of all arrogance and pretence.

She would have liked to say something soft and gentle to let him know that she understood, but her instincts told her that this was the last thing he would want.

In a cool, detached voice she said, 'Well, thank goodness you're getting some professional advice about the condition. It's quite tricky to deal with; there are so many facets that have to be considered, and in the end I believe it comes down very much to individual approach.'

He asked sharply, 'Have you come across this condition before?'

'Yes,' she replied calmly, 'twice.'

'Well, I'm damned! You really are something rather special, Miss Emma Seymour, are you not?'

'If you say so, sir,' she said with a dimpling smile.

He chuckled and asked so unexpectedly that she blushed, 'Have you got dimples, Emma?' and when she didn't answer at once, aptly guessed again, 'I do believe you're blushing!'

This man, she thought, is far too perceptive, with or without his sight. He must have been a formidable character a few months ago, with all his powerful faculties going full blast. A man, as well as a surgeon, to be reckoned with. A plastic surgeon of great repute, and only now in his late thirties. Immediately she'd known that she might be going to work for him she had acquired a couple of books that he'd written several years earlier. These had been about plastic surgery in general, and the psychological as well as physical benefits of surgery.

For some reason she had been surprised by his intuitive and gentle understanding of patients' needs, concerned with looks as much as medical necessity.

'Why shouldn't a lady of sixty, suddenly faced with the scarring effect of excision of a facial ulcer, receive the same cosmetic treatment as a girl of seventeen?' he had written. He had made other remarks as enlightened and sympathetic, which Emma had found endearing.

Now, looking at the embittered man before her, she wondered if he still felt the same. How ironic that his injuries and subsequent illness had deprived him of the ability, at least at present, to carry on with his work. And, she wondered, how badly scarred was his own face around the eyes? Could he benefit from the skilled plastic surgery that he himself had performed on others?

Her heart was full of compassion, and a great desire to help this man recover his health and skill overwhelmed her. She would, she knew, put up with his temper, perhaps at times total hostility.

She would suggest and, with his GP's help, start a regime of care that would set him on the road to recovery. A feeling of great confidence in her ability to help the professor engulfed her. Nothing he would say or do would deter her from her goal.

Mrs Mac came to the door of the study to announce

that lunch was ready, so saving Emma the embarrassment of replying to the professor's comment about blushing.

'Will you fetch my stick for me, Emma?' he asked politely and rather to her surprise. 'On this route, across the hall and down stairs, I need it.'

She collected the elegant ebony stick, trimmed with brass rings—or could they be gold? she wondered—beneath the curved handle, from beside his armchair, and handed it to him. He stood up, leaning heavily on his cane, and towered over her.

'Let's away to lunch, Miss Seymour,' he said, his voice once more ringing with sarcasm. 'You will please lead the way.'

His changes of mood would be hard to take, she thought, but somehow she would learn to accept or ignore them and concentrate on his well-being.

He paused as they passed the paino, and ran the fingers of his free hand over the keys.

'Do you play, Miss Seymour?'

'Yes, a little, for my own pleasure. Do you play, Professor?'

'Yes, a little, for my own pleasure,' he mimicked, 'but I prefer the pipes.' He paused for effect. 'I don't suppose, Miss Emma Seymour, that your perfections run to playing the pipes?'

With difficulty and tremendous self-control, she kept her cool.

'I've never tried, Professor. Is it difficult to play the pipes?'

He roared with laughter.

'You're determined not to take umbrage at my childish intemperance, Emma. Isn't that so?'

'Well, you said it, Professor.'

He seemed to be restored to good humour, which lasted throughout the meal. As at dinner last night, he changed his spectacles for a pair that had a transparent though powerful lens over his partially sighted eye. This enabled him to cope with his food unaided, though it did not appear to be very comfortable. Now, as then, he kept his head bent so that she was only able to catch a glimpse of his eye, and that at an angle. Not until she treated his eyes under Dr MacLeod's supervision that afternoon would she see them properly.

Angus was visiting friends. Emma and the professor lunched alone, off delicious poached salmon and salad, followed by lemon tart, a Mrs Mac speciality, and her home-made ice-cream. It was a relaxed occasion, with James maintaining his cheerful mood, playing the perfect host, relating stories about local people and places.

The effort, though, clearly tired him. He was obviously relieved to change his glasses again for his dark pair. In spite of the swift exchange that he contrived with his long, sure surgeon's fingers, Emma noticed that both eyes looked very sore and puffy.

Knowing from Angus that he was supposed to rest for an hour after lunch, she excused herself to explore the garden and sea-shore. She promised to be back by three, when Dr MacLeod was expected.

In the event, he arrived early and found her in the garden among the heady scent of the roses.

'It's got to be Miss Seymour,' he said, advancing with outstretched hand, 'unless Mrs Mac has completely metamorphosed.' His voice was that of the other Highlanders she had so far met, soft and sibilant with gently rolling Rs, educated, but less anglicised than those of the MacDonald family of doctors.

'Dr MacLeod, I presume,' replied Emma in equally bantering fashion.

They liked each other on sight. Emma thought that the sturdy man in his fifties looked very fit, very kind and totally reliable. He was just the support that she needed to care for her difficult but charismatic patient. His greying hair and matching neat beard and moustache were complemented by an old-fashioned suit of khaki-coloured cotton, an open-necked silk shirt, and loosely folded Paisley cravat. He looked like an actor out of a Second World War jungle film.

Dr MacLeod thought the slender silver-haired girl with fabulous green eyes who came to meet him, speaking in a husky, gentle voice, was exactly what James needed to shake him out of his misery. If she was as efficient as she was beautiful she was just what the doctor ordered, he decided with an inward grin at his pun. Unknowingly he too thought, as Angus had, that it was a pity his friend couldn't see this lovely girl properly.

They sat in one of the little arbours that were dotted around the garden, and Mrs Mac, who had seen the doctor's arrival from a window, appeared with a jug of iced lemonade and two tall glasses.

'Now, chust you sit there and cool off,' she ordered, 'before you go in and take up the cudgels with Master Jamie.'

When she had returned to the house Dr MacLeod made a face.

'Oh, dear,' he said, 'I'm afraid "Master Jamie" in that tone means that James is in a bad temper. How was he this morning?'

'Fine—well, most of the time, and certainly he was

very happy at lunchtime. Perhaps he over-tired him-self—he made a great effort to entertain me.'

'This, of course, is the result of his infection, plus sheer frustration at his disability.' He turned to look at Emma and give her a beaming smile. 'You'll not hold them against him, Miss Seymour, will ye, now, these tantrums that he's given to?'

'Why, of course not, Doctor. I'm a nurse, and both Angus and Dr Philippa warned me of his uncertain temper.' She laughed. 'In fact, the professor himself warned me about it.'

'Aye, that would be James,' replied the doctor, looking relieved at her reaction. 'He can take a good, hard look at himself as well as at others.'

'A bit of a Professor Higgins-type character,' mused Emma, and then blushed violently as she realised that she'd spoken aloud.

Dr MacLeod looked thoughtful, and then replied, 'Oh, aye, so he is, then, so he is.'

They sat in the shady fragrant rose bower and discussed the professor's treatment.

'You know his eyes are being looked after by Sir Hugh Robertson,' said Dr MacLeod. Emma nodded. 'He's the best eye man north of the border, probably south as well. He's based in Edinburgh, but has a cottage up here and visits James from time to time. He would fly up at once if there was an emergency. They go back a long way, and he has reason to be grateful to James for putting his wife's face back together again after an accident.'

Emma murmured something appropriate. The pro-fessor would obviously have high-powered colleagues in the medical world, but he seemed to have many devoted friends too. What an enigma of a man. Of course, his condition made him irritable, but she felt that even at his fittest he might be a difficult man to please, yet it hadn't lost him friends apparently.

Dr MacLeod was saying, 'The irrigation with normal saline should be done before and after swabbing to both eyes with the special lotion that Sir Hugh has prescribed. Gentamicin drops to both eyes, and similar ointment to the lids of his partially sighted eye. This eye we have to watch carefully in case a fungal infection occurs. If in doubt withhold treatment and let me know immediately.'

'Of course, Doctor. What about the area round each eye? I glimpsed them at lunchtime when the professor changed his glasses, and they looked very sore and swollen.'

'Yes, they are. He has several purely soothing ointments and creams to treat them with. I should let him guide you over that. It's a question of comfort, and what suits him one day may not the next.'

'Right, that sounds sensible. Now, what about his post-viral fatigue? I understand that a friend of his is planning some treatment, but is there anything that you want me to do in the meanwhile?'

'Ah, yes, this modern phenomenon that my granny used to refer to as the body being drained after being in battle. Nature's way of telling you to take a rest, go away and lick your wounds.' The doctor leaned forward and tapped Emma on the arm. 'Viruses were there, you know, Nurse, before we discovered them hiding in the laboratory. Our fathers and forefathers knew about them. Medical men at the turn of the century would tell their wealthy patients to go on a cruise. Poor devils who couldn't do that were advised to take some time off work, and given a certificate to prove that they needed it.'

Emma was for a moment shattered. She had thought that Dr MacLeod, in spite of his old-fashioned appearance, would be an ally; but the way he was talking about this important syndrome, so recently acknowledged by the less blinkered members of the medical profession, seemed derisory.

He saw the look on her face and smiled reassuringly. 'I'm on your side, my dear. I believe in a period of rest and recuperation after a serious or acute illness. Neither did I need convincing by my peers in the profession that some patients suffer from an inability to get back into their stride after surgery. My mother used to say everyone needed a bit of coddling after being ill. Together with many of her generation, she knew that flu was a six-week job—none of your forty-eight-hour stuff—two weeks incubating and feeling rough, two weeks of high temperature, thirst and headache, and two weeks to convalesce. She was right, you know, and just because we now have antibiotics to deal with the infection it doesn't mean that the body can take a beating without a breather.'

'Well, I never!' exclaimed Emma, bowled over by his passionate declamation. It was a silly thing to say, but she couldn't think of a more sensible reply.

The doctor stood up. 'Sorry, my dear, bit of a hobby-horse of mine. I suppose I like to think that on this one issue at least I'm way ahead of my cleverer colleagues. As I'm just a humble GP it does wonderful things for my ego.' He smiled amiably, a different man from the passionate advocate of a moment before.

Emma, having recovered her usual cool, laughed.

'My goodness, to think I was under the impression that you needed convincing!' she said.

'I think we're going to get along very well, Miss Seymour, to the benefit of our patient.'

They went into the house and found the professor in his study. He turned an angry face towards them as they entered.

In a sarcastic voice he asked, 'Been ganging up on me, Hector?'

'Now, why should I do that with your charming nurse who's only here to do her best for you?'

The professor looked at once contrite. 'I'm sorry—apologies, apologies, Emma, and you too, Hector.'

Mrs Mac appeared with a tray of tea. 'Ach, he's like a bear with a sare head.' She put the tray on a side-table. 'You'll pour, Miss Seymour, nae doot.'

'Of course.'

'Just ring if you want more scones.'

Mrs Mac left the room.

Emma didn't want tea or scones, and neither, she was sure, did the professor. They would both have liked to get on with the treatment session, but Dr MacLeod was clearly looking forward to Mrs Mac's delicacies. He polished off most of the scones, and drank two cups of tea to their one, before making a move towards the cloakroom opening off the study.

This had been neatly adapted for the purpose in hand. It contained a medical chair with a swivelling head-rest, which could be tilted at the correct angle. Standing beside it was a covered trolley laden with all that would be needed for eye and ulcer dressings.

Another, 'dirty', trolley holding plastic bins stood ready to receive cast-off dressings and implements. A wall-cupboard with a shelf attached contained stock dressings, ointments, bottles of various liquids, forceps, syringes and scissors. Everything to facilitate the professor's care had been provided.

Emma stationed herself behind the chair in which the professor had seated himself. Under Dr MacLeod's instructions, she removed the dark glasses and, from the left eye, a padded dressing. Both eyes were gunged up with a sticky exudation. She swabbed it away with the special cleaning and antiseptic fluid prescribed by Sir Hugh, and gently prised the lids apart.

She had wondered about the colour of the professor's eyes, and now she discovered that they were violet, almost to the point of blackness. Was the partial sightedness responsible for this? she wondered. The pupils of both eyes seemed undamaged, though she knew that one eye was, as it were, hanging by the thread of the undamaged part of the optic nerve. If that went, sight went.

Treatment had so far kept the portion of the nerve working. It was up to her to maintain the status quo and improve it by nursing care. Well, she would do her damnedest. Nothing she would do or fail to do would prevent his regaining full sight in that eye. The other less badly damaged eye was responding well to treatment. The cornea, as with the other eye, and the surrounding tissues had been damaged, but the pupil was unaffected. Time and care should put that right.

She finished the applications to both eyes and recovered them as instructed, and then turned her attention to the ulcerated leg.

The dressing that was designed to remain *in situ* for several days was removed. Both the professor and Dr MacLeod were pleased with the improvement.

Greatly daring, Emma suggested, 'As I'm here all

the time, couldn't we leave the dressing off for much
of the day and expose the ulcer to the sun? I could
cover it at any time should it be necessary.'

'Why not?' asked the professor.

'I'm not sure,' said Dr MacLeod. 'It's only recently
started to granulate.' The professor made a snorting
sound of derision, and the doctor held up a hand in
reproof. Then, realising that this patient couldn't see
his hand, he said firmly, 'I'm your GP, James. If you
want me to remain so, I'll make the decision.' He
sounded very fierce and sure of himself, and, though
Emma didn't agree with him, she admired his forthright
way of making it plain that he was in charge. 'We'll
consider Miss Seymour's suggestion on my next visit.'
He turned to Emma. 'It's a good idea; I just need time
to think about it.'

The professor was surprisingly meek, evidently
recognising the doctor's right to say his piece.

'But you will consider it, then?' he asked.

'Certainly, James. Just give me a breathing-space.'

Dr MacLeod left soon after this. Emma saw him off.

'I think your idea a good one,' he told her again,
'but James must understand that other people are
controlling his treatment at this time.' Emma made a
face. 'I'm not just being dog in the manger; psychological factors count too, you know. In a way, he'll be
comforted by the fact that others know what's best for
him, and respond accordingly. The problem of being a
patient when one has always been on the giving and
not the receiving end of the medical spectrum is that of
authoritative guidance.'

Emma blinked. She had thought that Dr MacLeod
was an elderly, rather retrogade medical man and that
psychology was outside his ken. Now she knew better.

He would be her ally in the fight to restore the professor to his pinnacle of fame and expertise. Together they would succeed. Of this she was suddenly and overwhelmingly certain.

'Goodbye,' she said, 'until your next visit.'

'Goodbye,' said the doctor. 'We understand each other, I think.'

'Oh, yes,' she said softly, 'we do.'

# CHAPTER THREE

ANGUS arrived back that evening from visiting his
friends. He, the professor and Emma had a hilarious
time over a magnificent dinner provided by Mrs Mac.
The professor was as hospitable as he had been at
lunchtime, a perfect host, but now more relaxed.
Emma thought that he was probably as relieved as she
to have got his first treatment over.

After dinner they all three strolled in the rose
garden, inhaling the delicious scents arising from the
extravagant blooms and the nicotianas planted between
the roses. Their soft, sweet perfume wafted around the
garden and drenched the arbour at which they eventually came to rest.

'Back at work tomorrow, Angus,' said the professor
to his brother.

'Yes, I'll return to the mainland by the afternoon
ferry.'

'Emma can drive you in the Range Rover. I might
come too.'

Why, thought Emma, does it seem like a challenge?
Is the professor going to test my driving skills? It had
been one of the preferred requirements for the post as
secretary-nurse, though not mentioned in the original
advertisement. A clean driving licence and ability to
drive well, Dr Philippa MacDonald had said. Emma
had been happy to confirm that she complied on both
counts.

'I've driven over very difficult terrain in ambulances,'

she had explained, 'when I did a stint for the WHO.' She hadn't gone into details, but had recalled to herself a journey made over rugged country in a vehicle carrying half a dozen wounded from a war zone to safety.

It seemed odd recalling this event in the calm and sunshine of a Skye summer's evening, especially in the sweet-scented garden of the MacDonalds' home.

Dr Philippa had been impressed.

'The problem is, my brother is a first-class driver. Since his accident, and with his blindness, he's become acutely aware of being driven by poor or inexperienced drivers. I'm afraid that he's quite Draconian in his assessment of those who drive him.' She had gone on to say that, in fairness, should an applicant meet all the other requirements, but not be a faultless driver, he would consider that person. There were locals who could drive at least reasonably well and who knew the terrain. Emma, confident of her ability to drive a heavy or four-wheel-drive vehicle, had had no hesitation in saying so.

Had that, she now wondered, been the deciding factor in appointing her as secretary-nurse to the professor?

'I'll be delighted to drive you, Angus, and the professor anywhere, as necessary,' she said now.

'You've picked up the gauntlet,' said the professor, with what Emma decided was a sneer in his voice.

'If you mean that I have by saying that I'll drive you anywhere, under more or less any conditions, then yes, Professor, I have picked up the gauntlet.'

'Bravo, well done!' said Angus enthusiastically.

In a quieter manner, the professor endorsed his

brother's enthusiasm. 'You've done some driving for the WHO,' he said, 'according to Philippa.'

'Yes, I have.'

'Well, I don't think we can better that. I shall be only too pleased to put myself in your hands, Emma.'

'Bully for you,' retorted Emma, knowing that her credentials were impeccable, and halfway resenting the idea that she was being tested.

'As you say,' replied the professor mildly, sounding so reasonable that Emma felt foolish for having made her sarcastic remark.

Angus glanced from one to the other of them rather anxiously.

'I say, don't spoil a perfect evening by being scratchy with each other!'

Simultaneously, both Emma and the professor protested, 'I'm not scratchy!'

They burst out laughing when they realised that they had spoken in unison, and any friction that had begun ceased instantly.

'What about a walk along the shore?' suggested the professor. 'And why don't you two have a swim before the smudgies really get going?'

'Smudgies?' asked Emma.

'Midges, we call them smudgies hereabouts. They're perfect pests. Come in swarms in the evenings, particularly as the sun sets. We've been lucky so far this evening, but they'll soon put in an appearance.'

They went back through the house, and Emma and Angus disappeared upstairs to change while the professor waited for them in the sitting-room.

What an awful shame that the professor couldn't go swimming, thought Emma. It would have done him the world of good, reducing the stress and tiredness caused through the ME syndrome, as well as simply being a pleasure. She began to think of ways and means by which he might go into the water once his leg ulcer was healed sufficiently. Surely they could between them make sure that his eyes were not contaminated?

She arrived back downstairs to find the two men waiting for her on the terrace. She had draped a short towelling robe round her shoulders over a black one-piece costume. In the latest fashion, this was shaped high over her slender hips and low between her small breasts, and lower still at the back, where it moulded itself over her firm buttocks. It was, she suddenly realised, sexier than her skimpy bikini, though super-ficially it might appear more modest.

She made to pull her robe closer about her as she noted Angus's frankly admiring gaze followed by a low wolf-whistle.

'Contain yourself, Angus,' said the professor in a reproving elder-brotherly voice, though his lips were quirking at the corners at what he couldn't see but could imagine. 'Emma will be thinkng we're unres-trained, chauvinistic Celts without any breeding at all!'

Emma decided to be joking about the situation.

'And what makes you think, Professor, that I haven't already reached that conclusion?' she asked sweetly, with a smile that he could hear in her voice.

He replied with mock horror, 'Don't say we've given ourselves away already, Miss Seymour?'

'All right,' she replied cheekily, 'I won't say it.'

She made a rush from the terrace to the beach, followed hotfoot by Angus, only halting when the professor called out in a plaintive voice, 'Isn't anybody going to spare a thought for a blind man?'

The words struck her like a splash of cold water on her hot skin.

'Oh, how dreadful,' she panted to Angus as he caught up with her. 'We didn't think about the professor.'

Angus hooted with laughter.

'James,' he said firmly, 'could beat you to the shore any time. He's just putting on an act. Look, he's down from the terrace already, and it's a clear path, as he knows, to the shore.'

'He seems to remember where everything is.'

'He does. He's got a fantastic memory, as you'll learn when you start helping him put his lectures together into book form. Even this wretched ME doesn't seem to have affected that.'

The professor joined them in no time. Angus was quite right; he had found his way down to the sandy shore without difficulty, and very quickly. He had, though, kept on the glasses that he used when eating, which meant that he could see something out of one eye.

This knowledge made Emma feel vulnerable, for some reason. She could accept that Angus found her attractive and sexy in the black costume over her pale, creamy golden tan, but the idea that the professor, even with his limited vision, could examine her she found disturbing.

After a while she pretended to shiver in the silky warmth of the clear water.

'I must go in and have a shower,' she said, reluctantly stepping out of the shallows on to the beach and reaching for her robe.

'What a pity,' said the professor, with an 'I know why you're really going' tone in his voice. 'The

Northern Lights, or aurora borealis, should be visible later.'

'Then I shall return,' replied Emma. She didn't add that she would by then be fully dressed.

'Do, Miss Seymour, do,' said her host and employer jovially, and seeming to read her thoughts, which he found amusing.

Half an hour later she returned to the shore. The 'smudgies' were out in force. Great clouds of them attacked her as she made her way down the path. She had smothered cream supplied by Mrs Mac on her hands and face, the only parts of her now exposed. At Mrs Mac's suggestion she had put on an all-enveloping cotton jump-suit and jammed a battered straw hat found for her by the housekeeper over her silver hair.

Showering and changing had taken longer than intended. She wasn't even sure if either of the brothers would be there, still at the water's edge, but they were.

Angus had put on a tracksuit, and the professor had added a 1930s cardigan over the pristine white shirt that he'd worn at dinner. He'd also donned a soft, almost shapeless felt hat and bright cravat. This made him look like a handsome spy straight out of a Bond movie, even similar to the other James himself, except that the MacDonald variety was darker and leaner.

'We're going to light a fire on the outcrop beneath the rowan tree and sit there for the display if it comes,' explained Angus. The professor was already making his way towards the rocks, and Angus put out a hand to slow Emma down to a dawdle behind him. 'You look fabulous,' he murmured. 'That green suit matches your eyes.'

Emma dimpled and was glad that she'd forked out some of her small reserves of cash to go mad on a shopping spree just before journeying north. Her wardrobe was still pretty meagre, but she had acquired one or two good quality items that were apparently pleasing. She surprised herself by briefly and quite fiercely wishing that the professor could see her properly. He might not pay her easy compliments—that wasn't his style—but he would make considered and apt comments that she could believe. Mild praise from him would be more valuable than another man's more fulsome words.

Angus pulled her close to him and very gently kissed her on the cheek.

'You're a lovely girl, Emma. James is a lucky guy to have you with him all day and every day. I envy him.'

'You can't mean that, Angus. He's blind—well, nearly so—and ill. That's a ridiculous thing to say. How can you envy him?'

She was astonished by her own agitation, not by Angus's kiss. That had been innocent enough, and she'd experienced many kisses that were anything but in her time. It was the way he had spoken of James that bothered her. His words had been said with conviction. He'd meant what he'd said. He was obviously very attracted to her. Strange that the very gentleness of his approach underlined something more than mere physical attraction.

The fact that they'd only met two days previously was of little account. Emma only had to recall how hopelessly and utterly she had fallen in love at first sight with Ricky Elliot, when as a junior registrar he had given her block group ENT lectures, to accept that this was a possibility. The only difference was that Ricky had returned her passion, whereas she had only friendly feelings for Angus.

She and Ricky had been inseparable for months. She had been desperately hurt when he had moved on to another hospital as a senior registrar and dropped her like a hot potato. Her aunt, she knew, had been partly responsible for his sudden lack of interest, though she had never known what she had said or done to precipitate matters. But only later had she discovered that he had taken up with the daughter of the ENT professor at his new teaching hospital. That had really hurt. Though plain and of a rather unprepossessing character, she was patently a much better catch, professionally, than Emma.

All these thoughts rushed through her mind as she and Angus stood together, hand in hand, on the beach.

Angus said, stumbling over his words, 'I don't, of course, mean that I envy James his situation, only that I envy him the months ahead with you as a constant companion.' He gripped her hand so hard that she almost cried out. 'For once, Emma, I might have the first bite of the cherry.' He saw that she looked bewildered. 'I mean that James has always collared all the girls. Odd, but we both seem to be attracted to the same type of girl. Up to now I've always backed off right from the word go. I haven't been able to compete with him, except back in Inverness at my own hospital—my own stamping ground, you see. But here, now, with you, I feel that I may have a chance.' He released her hand. 'Do I have a chance, Emma?' he asked wistfully.

She didn't want to hurt him.

'I like you very much, Angus. But it's a bit soon for anything more, don't you think?'

'Yes, of course—stupid of me. Are we still friends?'

'Why, of course. I shall miss you when you leave.'

'Well, that's something, I suppose.' He gave her an engaging grin. 'Will you come over to the mainland when my tyrannical brother gives you some time off?'

'Certainly.' She gave him a smile that seemed to satisfy him.

'That's great,' he said, just as the professor called out to ask if they were coming.

'Stop smooching!' he shouted in a commanding voice, as if he had seen Angus's kiss. 'And come and get this damned fire going, Angus.'

The knowledge that she was anxious for her employer's approval in matters outside of work niggled away at Emma for much of the evening. It was annoying to think that the professor already seemed to have exerted an influence over her, especially as his behaviour had been so volatile since her arrival.

She sat between the two men, waiting for the Northern Lights to appear. Angus kept glancing at her anxiously, as if he expected her to say or do something connected with their recent conversation. The professor, who might or might not have intercepted any vibes that were about, kept up a continuous flow of conversation.

'Do you know anything about the aurora?' he asked Emma.

'Only what I've read or was told at school, and once, when I was a small child, my father took me into the garden to see it.'

'Where was that?'

'The Isle of Wight, just about as far south as one can get to see it, I believe.'

'No, it's possible even in France or Spain, but very infrequently and, of course, not so brilliantly as here or Scandinavia.'

'Oh, I didn't realise that. In fact, I'm really terribly stupid about what causes it and so on.'

The professor turned his head towards her as Angus moved away to throw some more branches on the lazily smoking fire.

He said softly, 'I don't really believe that you're stupid about anything, Emma. I think you are as clever as you are beautiful, and only ignorant about facts that haven't been important to you.'

Angus moved back from the fire and sat down again beside her. Emma struggled to quell her surprise at the professor's words. He carried on talking as if nothing untoward had been said.

'The aurora,' he said, 'are formed when charged particles emitted by the sun are caught by the earth's magnetic field and focused down on to the atmosphere, causing it to glow, rather like a television screen.'

'You sound like a bloody professor giving a lecture,' said Angus in a teasing sort of manner.

'Well, perhaps that's because I am one.' He turned again to Emma. 'Sorry, my dear, I don't mean to bore you.'

'You're not, not in the least.'

'See?' said the professor to his brother, grinning like a schoolboy.

'She's only being polite,' replied Angus, still kidding.

'Are you just being polite?' asked James.

'No, of course not,' she replied, joining in the laughter and thinking what a wonderful rapport the brothers had with each other.

Dusk began to fall and a sudden curtain of grey appeared on the horizon, stretching from east to west.

'Oh!' she exclaimed, disappointed. 'It's gone dark. Does that mean the Lights won't appear after all?'

'Quite the opposite,' said James cheerfully. 'Watch the dark horizon and presently you'll see an arch of colours. If we're lucky there may be a boreal crown or corona, as it's sometimes called. That's a crown of lights, usually red and green, sitting on spirals of other colours.' Casually he reached out a hand and clasped hers. 'Tell me what you see,' he murmured softly.

Emma's heart was thudding uncomfortably, partly because of his hand holding hers, partly because she had for a moment forgotten that he could not see, and was suddenly stricken with remorse at having forgotten. Angus was absorbed in watching the north-western sky.

'The dark cloud seems to be breaking up at the corners,' she said, 'and a ribbon of light is spiralling up from the centre. It's a beautiful metallic green and cinnamon red. It's spreading into an arch with other colours, and fountains of colour are bursting up from the horizon. Oh, James, it must be the crown—it's absolutely fantastic!'

It had come out so naturally that she hadn't even noticed that she'd said his name. The professor tightened his grip on her hand.

'Thanks, dear Emma, for lending me your eyes,' he said softly.

'My pleasure,' she replied, tears gathering in her own at the thought of his blindness.

The spectacle of the aurora lasted for some time. At last it began to fade, the colours becoming more muted and blurred, finally coming to rest on what looked like the top of the world in a band of smoky reds and greens. The near-full moon rose, silvering the sea, the shore and the rowan tree beneath which they sat.

Angus doused the fire and the three of them walked

quietly up the beach to the house, awed by the majesty of the blazing display they had just witnessed.

There seemed to be little to say when they arrived in the sitting-room. By common consent they decided to go to bed.

'Will you have a nightcap, Emma,' asked the professor, 'before you go up?'

She was about to refuse, when the phone rang, and Angus moved to answer it. The call was for him, apparently.

'Hold on,' he said to the caller, and to Emma and James, 'I'll say goodnight and take this in my room. Will you hold on, Emma, until I get up there?'

He looked a little embarrassed, she thought, and realised why when a breathless female voice said, 'Angus, darling!' when he picked up the receiver in his room. She replaced the receiver at her end and turned to meet the professor's sardonic grin.

'Ah, my little brother and one of his *amours*.' He laughed, but it was a gentle, kindly laugh. 'Angus has a marvellous way with the lassies.'

For a moment she was tempted to repeat what his brother had said about him and his amatory successes, but the moment passed.

'Will you have a drink, Emma?' he asked again.

Her heart thundered at the thought of being alone with him in the intimacy of the softly lighted room.

'What would you recommend, Professor, as a nightcap after such an exciting evening?' She was thinking of the aurora, but blushed at the thought that he might read something else into her remark.

'Brandy, a good brandy,' he replied. 'A most civilising drink. Great for calming the nerves and putting things back in perspective.' His voice dropped to a low, husky key. 'Do you mind pouring, dear girl? I still haven't mastered the art of making a good job of that.'

Emma felt that she wasn't making too good a job of it either. Her hands were shaking, and the glasses clinked as she rattled the decanter against them. The professor was standing just behind her, not crowding her, but when she turned to hand him his glass he was less than an arm's length away.

She tried to tame her uneven breathing as she guided his hand to the glass. He took it from her easily, with cool, firm fingers that just touched hers.

'Take your glass, Emma,' he said, 'and let's toast our future, for however long or short that might be. I fancy that you and I are going to enjoy working together.'

They touched their balloon glasses together, and it seemed to Emma that it meant more than the kiss on the cheek that Angus had given her earlier that evening. She could feel the heat from the professor's body as their glasses met, and her own skin tingled at their closeness.

This, she thought, is madness. But when he stretched out his free hand and touched her she moved closer still.

He mumbled something about putting these damned glasses down, and she placed her own, and then his, on a side-table. It seemed the most natural thing in the world that he should gather her into his arms, and that she should hold up her face to be kissed, and kiss his lips in return.

An untold time later he gently eased her away from him.

'I'm sorry, dear girl, I didn't mean that to happen,' he murmured.

Emma stood at a little distance from him and smoothed her jump-suit straight.

'What's a little kiss?' she asked flippantly, determined to disguise her mixture of panic, excitement and surprise. What on earth had happened?

'A kiss? Nothing, or perhaps everything,' replied the professor enigmatically. He turned from her and with searching fingers found his glass where she had put it on the small table. 'Whatever, here's to us, Emma.'

Emma picked up her glass. 'To us,' she echoed, and drained the smooth liquid at one go. She started towards the door, and then turned back. 'Do you need help, Professor, to get to your room?' Deliberately she made her voice cool and efficient.

'I can manage fine, thank you. Goodnight, and thank you for a pleasant evening.'

Emma fled upstairs to her room, her mind a jumble of sad and happy thoughts, which no way could she unravel before sleep overtook her.

She went down to breakfast as late as she dared, hoping that both the brothers might have finished and departed elsewhere. They were both there, and both half rose from their chairs as she entered the room.

'Please,' she said, motioning them to resume their seats, and thinking that one couldn't fault them on their manners, whatever their amatory inclinations. She added a 'Good morning', to which they responded, and collected cereals and toast from a side-table.

'Coffee?' asked Angus, giving her a warm and conspiratorial smile tinged with concern. He was clearly wondering what her reaction had been or might be to last night's phone call. He, of course, knew nothing of the sequence of events that had occurred with his brother.

'Please.' Her staccato reply brought a smile to the professor's lips, but he made no direct comment.

He said in his usual detached manner, quite obliterating last night's episode, 'Angus was reading my letters to me, something that will fall to you after today, Emma.'

'Of course; I realised that would be a secretarial chore.' To her amazement, her voice sounded much as usual, cool and slightly husky, but without any overtones of intimacy or surprise.

'Good. I have very few intimate or personal letters, as obviously my family and close friends, aware of my blindness, confine themselves to phone calls. There should be nothing in my daily mail to embarrass either of us.'

His tone and words sounded to Emma's heightened receptors rather sarcastic, as if he was warning her that, though he had confidential matters to consider, he had no intention of her being party to them.

Angus looked embarrassed, a state that he easily fell prey to, with his fair skin and reddish hair.

'You're being bloody rude again, James,' he said in an angry voice.

'No, I'm not. Emma knows exactly what I mean, and will be relieved to know that she won't have to handle personal mail.'

It was just over a week later before they both found out how prophetically wrong he was.

That afternoon Emma drove Angus and the professor to Armadale, from where the ferry crossed to Mallaig. The professor was a model passenger, sitting beside

her as she drove over the rough track that joined
MacDonald's Bay with the only slightly less rough road
to Kilbeg. This in turn linked up with the Armadale
road, and civilisation.

Just as earlier that day he had succumbed cheerfully
to her administering his treatment, so he sat quietly
letting her get on with the driving. She had rather
dreaded this first testing of her motoring ability, not
because she feared to fail, but because of the sarcastic
remarks, sparked off by a genuine anxiety, that the
professor was likely to make.

She was an imaginative as well as an efficient nurse,
and didn't find it difficult to understand the unpleasant
sensation that a blind person might feel of being
accelerated forward. Even wheelchairs took some getting used to, the blind patients at St Dunstan's had told
her.

It seemed sensible to talk their way through the first
precipitous part of the journey, telling him when they
were about to take a sharp bend, or traverse a particularly narrow piece of track. When they eventually came
out on to the smooth road to Armadale she stopped
talking, and the professor thanked her in a nice,
pleasant voice for her help.

'A neat progress report,' he said. 'Much appreciated.'

Angus said very little, either on the journey or before
they left, though this was partly because Emma had
avoided him. She had no desire to be drawn into a
discussion about his lady caller of last night. He was
free to do what he wished. If anything, the fact that he
had girlfriends clamouring for his attention on the
mainland was a relief.

How serious he had been when declaring his interest
in her on the dusky shore of the bay, Emma was not

sure. She knew, however, that she felt only friendship for him, and anything more serious from his point of view would have been an embarrassment.

The professor and Emma stood on the shore and watched and waved as the ferry crossed the Sound of Sleat with Angus on board. Emma was both glad and sorry to see him depart. He had lightened the first few days of her stay on Skye, and served as a buffer between her and James. On the other hand, she was anxious to get on with the job that she had been engaged for, as secretary and nurse to the professor.

Now, she felt, they could return to the bay and begin their work proper.

It seemed that the professor felt the same.

'Do you want to stop for tea,' he asked as the ferry disappeared into the haze of heat hanging over the water, 'or return home?'

'Home, please,' she replied with a conviction that made him smile in a satisfied manner.

'So be it,' he said, with obvious relief.

They drove back the way they had come, mostly in companionable silence, occasionally broken, when they reached the rougher tracks, by Emma's commentary.

Mrs Mac was at the door to greet them.

'Now,' she said, 'tea and toast and ginger cake on the terrace, in ten minutes.'

'Lovely,' said Emma.

'Exactly as the doctor ordered,' said the professor, sounding happy and relaxed.

# CHAPTER FOUR

THE next few days passed surprisingly quickly and with little acrimony, rather to Emma's surprise.

For some reason she had expected the professor to be particularly sarcastic about her help, and even more resentful of it once Angus had left; but this was not the case. He submitted to her nursing care with good grace, even on her third morning, when his multiple vitamin injection was due, complimenting her on her expertise with a needle.

'Not easy to give painlessly,' he said in a relieved voice as Emma withdrew the large-bore needle from the upper and outer quadrant of his buttock. 'Especially this stuff in an oily base.'

She swabbed and massaged the area gently to disperse the large quantity of fluid that had been injected into the immediate muscle tissues. Even though he had been ill and undernourished for a period, the professor's muscles in his buttocks and thighs were still awesomely firm and controlled. So, Emma noticed as he stood and pulled up his trousers, were his biceps, bulging under the short sleeves of his thin cotton shirt.

His body didn't show the effects of severe illness, due largely to his tan, acquired in tropical climes. It was also obvious that he must have been supremely fit prior to injury and infection, and this further disguised his condition. Only his face, showing lines of pain and fatigue, suggested that he was a sick man, and, of course, the dark glasses concealing his damaged eyes.

Emma was pleased to notice that by the fourth day the puffiness round his eyes had reduced and the exudation of matter was less viscous and sticky. His sight as yet might not be making vast improvements, but superficially his eye condition was responding to her regular treatment.

Dr MacLeod visited and agreed that James could have his leg ulcer exposed for much of the day. 'You might venture into the sea in a few days' time, when granulation should be well advanced, provided that the area is covered with a waterproof dressing,' he announced casually, to James's delight. 'Be guided by this young lassie here,' advised the doctor, gobbling up Mrs Mac's delicious sandwiches and drinking a third cup of strong tea. 'I missed my lunch,' he explained by way of apology. 'And I was out on a maternity case early this morning, ye ken.'

Mrs Mac, in the process of delivering another pot of tea, tut-tutted and asked the professor, 'Shall I be getting the puir wee man a proper bite to eat? He must be rare famished.'

'The contents of the larder are yours to dispose of as you think fit, Mrs Mac. I'm sure that the good doctor, puir wee man that he is,' said the professor with a broad grin, 'could consume whatever you choose to set before him.'

To the surprise of them all, Dr MacLeod refused cooked food, though he crammed a large slice of fruit cake into his mouth as he stood up to leave.

'What with a surfeit of babies at this time, and the holiday camp just over the hill, I'm fair run off my feet. No time to do justice to your delectables, Mrs Mac.'

'What about you and Maggie coming over for a meal tomorrow evening?' asked James.

'Well, now, I'll nae doubt be on call since yon Hamilton's still away to the mainland, but I'd like that fine, and I know for sure that Maggie will be pleased to meet yon lovely nurse here.' He gave Emma a charming smile and a little bow, which she, dimpling, replied to with a curtsy. 'I'll get Maggie to ring and confirm our coming.'

'Maggie,' explained the professor after the doctor had left, 'is Hector's sister. She's a retired nurse and was a typical old-fashioned battleship of a matron at the infirmary in Glasgow before you or I were born.'

'Goodness, she sounds alarming!'

'Not a bit—you and she will get on fine together. You may be a modern young nurse compared to Maggie, Emma Seymour, but you're a streamlined version of a battleship if ever I saw one, just as determined to get your own way where nursing is concerned. You'll have much in common.'

Emma didn't argue; it was, presumably, a compliment.

Although the professor showed no signs of irritation with her presence, neither did he show any particular pleasure in her company. Certainly nothing in his manner endorsed the warm and intimate kiss and caress that he had bestowed upon her on the night of the aurora borealis display. It might never have happened. Had he, she wondered, simply reacted the way he had to prove that he was still a force to be reckoned with in spite of his current disabilities?

They slipped into a routine of breakfast, when Emma read the post to James, followed by his treatment and then work on his lecture notes—videos and tapes. It took a while to tidy all his work records into date file, since there were several boxes of documents and discs, covering a three-month period. Once they were sorted, however, work began in earnest.

First Emma would put up the video pictures of operations and photos of patients before treatment, and when she had described them James would make further remarks, which she noted to type or process later. Often there was a commentary by James, but sometimes this was recorded separately on a tape, and occasionally in scrawled notes, and these had to be annotated with the films.

One picture, a still photo, brought tears to Emma's eyes. It was of a small girl with hideously scarred and distorted features. She described the picture to James.

'Oh, yes,' he said in a detached voice, 'Marishna, a six-year-old child deliberately marred and sent begging.'

'Six?' replied Emma unbelievingly. 'She looks about three years old.'

'So would you, had you been undernourished from birth. Besides, the smaller and frailer a child looks, the more sympathy it attracts from visitors, especially Western visitors,' he continued tonelessly.

Emma hoped that he was trying to make his voice sound cool and distant. Surely he was not unmoved by the plight of this child?

'Who did it? Who disfigured her?'

'Her uncle.'

'Her uncle? How could he?'

'Oh, easily. No one thought any the worse of him. He'd taken in his sister and the child when the husband was killed in an accident. He'd done his bit, especially when the child was born a girl and with a birthmark.'

'How awful! How horrible! And what about the mother, how did she feel?'

'I don't know how she felt, but I do know that she didn't hold her brother's conduct against him. He'd given her and her child a home. He didn't have to. It was his right to treat both her and her child as he wished.'

Emma couldn't control her feelings for a moment. She had, of course, heard of such things, vague allusions, even hideous pictures in some of the more lurid newspapers, but these had always been distanced somehow by her not knowing anyone directly connected with the issue. Now, here, in the beautiful island of Skye in the middle of a gorgeous summer, as she talked to a civilised and, she hoped, caring man about a child that he had actually touched, the full horror of what was happening daily in some distant country moved her deeply.

She excused herself and left the room for a while to regain her composure, telling herself that this was no way for an experienced nurse to behave. All her training reminded her that she must not become too involved with a patient. She must remember this and translate it into her reaction now towards a child in the East who surely must mean less to her than patients she had nursed in the past. She had been able then to practise a kind of detachment; surely she could exercise this detachment now? How the professor would despise her if she allowed her feelings to interpose between her and her work—indeed, *his* work.

She returned to the study a short while later. The professor was sitting as she had left him, facing the window that he couldn't see, hands together as if in prayer, supporting his chin.

'I'm sorry about that,' said Emma. 'It just seems so heartless.'

'Life tends to be that, don't you think?' he replied.

'Yes, I suppose so.'

'You don't sound convinced. Yet, with your experience with the WHO, I'd have thought you would be inured.'

'It was different somehow, people at war. Just as hideous and cruel, but at least it was enemies fighting each other for a cause, however ridiculous it might seem to outsiders. This. . .this business with this little girl was quite deliberate and unnecessary.'

He was silent for a moment, and then he said, still in what she considered a cold, unfeeling voice, 'Perhaps it will help you to know that this child has had and is still having treatment. She's being looked after by the nuns in a convent near the city where we found her. Given time and the healing properties of the young, she'll turn out to be quite a catch in, say, ten years' time.'

There was nothing more to say after that. James went on to describe the initial plastic surgery that he had performed on Marishna and explain what would be done in follow-up surgery over a period of time.

He ended up by recording on the tape, 'We will examine this little girl in a few months' time and assess what her chances are for further treatment. Prognosis at this time, hopefully good.'

For the first time Emma thought that she detected a softer note in his voice, but she refrained from further comment.

It was clear to Emma from the start that James MacDonald was a magnificent surgeon and a fluent and interesting lecturer. In the afternoons she retired to a small room off the professor's study, designated her office, to process the morning's work; and she found herself spending some precious minutes enjoying the pictures of James in theatre greens. Since some of the videos were taken by amateurs, there were often shots of the professor and assistants scrubbing up and discussing the case to come.

She was able to view the man as he had been before his accident, without either mask of dark glasses or cane to support his injured leg. What a virile, good-looking specimen he was, and so self-assured. It was obvious that any theatre in which he was working, in any part of the world, was completely under his authority. Perhaps, Emma thought, 'spell' or 'charisma' might equally apply.

His eyes, fringed by long dark lashes that should have belonged to a woman, intrigued her most, for the simple reason that she was seeing them for the first time unmarred by injury. It was almost a shock to discover that they were the same dark, almost black eyes that she was treating daily. One shot on a video had caught him as he looked up and stared straight into the camera. Even at that distance and on film, his eyes seemed to penetrate with frightening precision, as if they were homing in on her most secret thoughts.

She chided herself on being stupid and behaving like a schoolgirl, and attacked her work with great energy.

They had fallen into the habit of an evening of wandering down to the shore after dinner, braving the smudgies to enjoy the late-summer evening air. Even without the stupendous brilliance of the aurora borealis, the sunsets were magnificent. Great streaks of red, gold and almond-green blazed across the western sky, where the mountainous Cuillins across the bay crouched like some humpbacked creature, their heads swathed in misty, glowing clouds, their feet in the water.

Emma looked forward to these walks. James was at his most relaxed then, satisfied usually by his day's work, which was progressing well, and replete after one of Mrs Mac's delicious dinners.

It was about ten days after her arrival on the island, and they were returning from their walk rather later than usual in the near dark of the short summer night, when James halted abruptly and stood with his head averted at a listening angle. They were in the middle of a discussion about the failing Health Service and whether there was a place for private medicine, when James put a finger to her lips.

'Shoosh,' he whispered. 'Someone's calling.'

Emma looked up and down the empty beach. 'There's no one about,' she said softly.

'Listen!'

They stood very close together, hardly daring to breathe as the usual sounds of twilight trickled through the silence. The softly rippling water washed up and down the sandy foreshore, and a cloud of smudgies hummed over a patch of seaweed. A cow began a long mournful moo, which broke the serenity and made Emma jump.

The professor placed an arm round her shoulders, and she was grateful for its weight and reassuring pressure, for suddenly the quiet summer evening had become oppressive, threatening.

'There, it's coming from the outcrop,' he murmured, and this time Emma heard it too, a faint voice quivering and weakly calling, 'Help!'

She shook off her feeling of dread and at the same

time tried to shake off his arm, but he simply tightened his grip.

'You're not going on ahead,' he said in a tone that brooked no argument. 'We don't know what the hell it's all about. We go together.'

His leg had improved dramatically, and, though he still carried a cane with him outside the house, it was more for orientating himself than for support. Now the general improvement in his physical condition, and the improvement in the sight of his better eye, became obvious. He stepped out along the sandy beach, with a sureness of movement that Emma, in the gathering dusk, found difficult to emulate.

Of course, he had known the bay all his life, and with his prodigious memory was able to cater for many obstructions without seeing them. There was the little burn, for instance, that rushed down from the sloping fields, suddenly dropping over a mini-cliff to the beach, dissecting the route back to the outcrop. Unerringly he stopped at the side of the burn, reached out with his stick to assess the distance, then placed his foot on the opposite bank and offered Emma a hand over the rushing water. He easily maintained his balance, and brought his other leg over effortlessly, to stand beside her on the opposite bank.

He took her arm again and they made their hurried way towards the rowan tree and the rocky outcrop.

There was a girl huddled, half sitting, half lying, against the tree. She was plainly in distress.

For the first time since James had laid a warning finger to her lips he was prepared to relinquish his lead. Emma realised that because of the dimmer light beneath the tree and bushes he could see less well, but it was as if he was also aware of some other influence that held him back.

The girl looked up.

'Oh, thank you! Oh, God, thank you!' she said in a tremulous voice as Emma made her way through the brambles and bracken over the rocks. Then she looked past Emma to where James stood quietly leaning against a rock. 'No. . .no! No men—please!' She raised herself up from her crouching position, and then let out a sort of subdued shriek and doubled up in pain.

'He's a doctor,' explained Emma in the coolest voice she could muster.

'I don't care who he is, I don't want him around!' The vehemence of her remark, allied to her obvious weakness, was surprising.

James spoke quietly. 'I'm going away, up the beach to the house over there. This lady's a nurse; she'll know what to do.' He moved down the rocky precipice. 'Emma, when you're ready, bring the young lady up. I'll alert Mrs Mac.'

How had he known, Emma asked herself later that night, that the girl had been raped, was terrified of men at that moment and only wanted another woman to help her? But he had, apparently. He had taken himself off, and a while later Mrs Mac had appeared with a blanket which she had placed round the girl's shoulders while she persuaded her to come up to the house.

Only when they were installed in James's study did Emma know for sure that the girl had been raped, because the girl told her, in a belligerent and fragmented fashion, what had happened. Yet some sixth sense must have altered James and advised him to take himself off. For the first time since her arrival on Skye

Emma felt less than capable of dealing with the situation. She was suddenly aware of the professor's true strength and medical authority.

Rape was not something she had come up against even in hospital. She dimly remembered a rape victim coming into Casualty in the early days of her training, but she had been too junior to be involved. On the gynae ward she had dealt with the after-effects of rape, but this nursing was divorced by time and distance from the actual attack.

With a tremendous effort she pulled herself together and made the girl comfortable, elevating her hips and legs slightly when she saw that she was bleeding heavily. She instructed Mrs Mac to fetch towels and to stay with her while she went to consult with the professor.

'The police are on the way,' he said as she came through the door to the hall where he had stationed himself. He was just putting down the phone. Then he asked gently, 'Are you all right, my dear?'

'I'm fine,' she said with more assurance than truth. 'But that poor girl!' Almost accusingly she said bitterly, 'You knew, didn't you, that she'd been raped. How did you know?' For the life of her she couldn't stop herself sounding resentful, as if he had done something wrong.

'Circumstance, reason, and instinct,' he replied quietly, 'confirmed by her reaction to the presence of a man.'

'Yes, of course,' Emma mumbled, ashamed of her own attitude towards him. 'I'm sorry; I don't know what's the matter with me.'

'I do,' he said softly, stroking her cheek with gentle fingers. She was tempted to ask him what he meant, but he gave her no opportunity. 'What have you done so far?' he asked, and Emma told him.

'Is she bleeding excessively?' he wanted to know.

'Well, rather more than I would have expected, but controllable with elevation. Her pulse is quite strong, though rapid. I don't think that there's any severe internal bleeding, but she's in general shock, of course. Could there be any other reason for the bigger bleed?'

'She might be pregnant—this attack might have precipitated a near-abortion. It might be a spontaneous though small haemorrhage from a ruptured vessel, but that would. . .' He broke off, obviously unwilling to say more.

Emma had herself well under control now, and said calmly, 'That would indicate a very violent attack.' She added, not sure if the information was of any value, 'I don't think she's inexperienced.'

'A slight mitigation, I suppose, though I don't imagine that poor girl thinks so. Has she any idea who attacked her?'

'I have the feeling that she does—I don't know why—but she says she couldn't see who it was.'

'Where did it happen?'

'She doesn't seem too sure about that either.'

'Well, the police will sort that one out, I don't doubt. They should be here soon, together with an ambulance and the police surgeon.'

Emma turned to return to the study. James put a hand on her shoulder and squeezed it gently.

'You're doing fine,' he said, 'but let me know if there's anything I can do. If the bleeding gets too much I can give her a coagulant. But otherwise, considering the state she's in, I'd better keep out.'

Emma looked up and gave a quivering smile. 'Oh,

James. Thank you,' she said softly. 'Thank you. . .'
She felt there was something else she should say, but
no words came.

'Don't worry,' he said gently, seeming to sense her
inner thoughts. 'Just go to your patient. I'll see you
later.'

She had no time for reflection on this exchange; the
next half-hour was buzzing with activity. The ambulance, police, and surgeon—a woman, Emma was
relieved to see—all turned up within minutes of each
other.

Mary Maguire, the surgeon, made a very superficial
examination before the patient was moved, deciding to
delay a more thorough one till later, in hospital.

'The girl is pregnant,' she told Emma and the
professor, 'but she hasn't aborted, thanks to your
elevating her limbs.' She smiled at Emma. 'Of course,
it will be touch and go, but I'm hopeful.'

'You'll let us know what happens, Mary?' asked
James as he and Emma stood in the porch, seeing the
little convoy off.

'Yes, of course, even if it means bending the rules a
bit.' The visiting doctor gave him a devastating smile
as she climbed into her Land Rover.

Yet another devoted admirer cum friend, thought
Emma as the professor closed the door on the still
night air, disturbed only by the humming of a cloud of
smudgies.

They returned to the study, where Mrs Mac was
endeavouring to tidy up.

'Here, let me help,' said Emma.

'I'll not hear of it, Miss Seymour; ye've done enough
for tonight, saving that wee lassie's bairn,' said the lady
indignantly. So Mrs Mac too had known that the girl

was pregnant. 'Away with ye both to the sitting-room, where ye'll find sandwiches and coffee. Surely Oona and I can finish off tomorrow fine.'

'I feel such a fool,' confessed Emma when she and the professor were comfortably ensconced in deep armchairs and munching sandwiches. 'Both you and Mrs Mac knew that the girl might be pregnant, but I didn't give that a thought until you suggested it.'

'Ah, but you did all the right things Emma. My dear, don't be distressed—both Mrs Mac and I have years of experience to guide us. It'll come to you in due course. I always think that training, experience and instinct go hand in hand. Make use of every piece of information that comes your way—that's the lesson I've learned.'

'You sound just like a consultant who retired soon after I started training; he said ask the granny in a family if you wanted to know more about a patient. Is that what you mean?'

'Exactly that. I've found that experience counts far more than anything else. Add that to academic knowledge and one has a slight chance of coming up with a possibly correct diagnosis.'

Emma found it strange that the professor, usually aloof on any personal level, should expand so much. Presumably he too was affected by the night's events. It made her bold enough to ask what he had meant when he'd said that he understood her anger with him earlier.

'Oh, Emma, we're not all monsters, you know, but I could quite see how you thought we were when you first realised what had happened to that girl. All men were anathema to you for the moment. Of course you wanted to take it out on the nearest male.' He looked infinitely sad. 'And why not? By and large, in this and

any other male-dominated species, the males are
responsible for most of the violence.'

For the third time, and again unwittingly, she used
his Christian name.

'Oh, James, if more men were like you. . .' Her
voice trailed away. A few hours earlier, in spite of the
improvement in their relationship, she would never
have credited him with being less than, especially
professionally, a male chauvinist. His caustic remarks
from the day of her arrival had seemed to mark him
out as this. He had been mostly polite after their first
few meetings, but always exuding his masculinity and
superiority. Even taking into account his sensitivity
over his blindness and other disabilities, she felt he had
remained aggressively male.

Now he seemed almost vulnerable, as a man and a
doctor. His already haggard face looked more so. His
one good eye, uncovered now, looked dull and lifeless,
and his brows were drawn almost together in an
unhappy frown.

It was hard to equate the man who sat opposite her
with the macho, though wounded, male of their first
meeting. He was clearly on the defensive, and she
longed to take the pressure off him.

She attempted to finish her unfinished sentence
briskly.

'If more men were like you, Professor, rape wouldn't
exist.'

He sprang out of his chair and was leaning over her
before she realised what had happened.

'Emma, the important thing to remember is that
there are more men around like me than of the other
kind. You must remember that. Most of my sex are
sickened by these happenings. Unfortunately, men

outside the medical and perhaps the church scene, and social workers and suchlike, are just not aware of how often this sort of situation occurs. Don't condemn us all, my dear, for those arrogant and depraved bastards who commit such crimes against women.'

It was a cry from the heart, and as astonishing as a thunderbolt, coming from the professor.

She found herself stammering a reply to this unexpected plea. 'I—I—d-don't! Of course most men aren't rapists, I never thought they were, but a lot of them make everyday living and working unpleasant for women.'

He said rather wearily, heaving himself back into an upright position, and walking across the room, 'Yes, I'm afraid we're most of us guilty of showing off when there's a female around. Old ingrained habits of centuries of domination die hard, Emma, the peacock in his plumage strutting around in front of the indifferent peahen in her drab brown.'

Perhaps because of her tiredness, and in spite of the serious conversation that they had been having, Emma found the picture that the professor had described very funny. She giggled. Uncontrollably the giggle turned into a splutter, and she reached for her handkerchief.

The professor was back at the side of her chair in a flash. 'Emma, what's wrong—are you choking?' He patted her gently on the back and then massaged the back of her neck with his long, strong fingers. 'Better?' he asked softly.

'It's heaven,' she replied, revelling in his electric touch, which was sending totally unexpected shock waves all over her. All the tenseness that the evening's events had produced drained away under the magic of his fingers firmly but gently pummelling her trapezius and deltoid muscles.

She could have sat there forever, letting him smooth away all the minor aches and pains of fatigue. Even without the extra thrill that his nearness was producing, it was fantastically comforting. Her common sense and duty took over, though, after a few minutes.

'Thanks,' she said in a grateful voice, which she struggled to keep cool. 'That's helped tremendously, but you must be tired too. I expect you want to get to bed—I know I do.' She eased herself away from the back of her chair and stood up. 'Thanks again.' She moved towards the door.

'Think nothing of it. Glad to have been of service. Like you, I'm ready for bed.' He was smiling, a gleam in his good eye, which had lost its earlier dullness.

He switched off the lamp on the nearby side-table and followed her from the room.

'Oh, Emma,' he murmured softly to himself as he trod quietly up the stairs behind her.

He climbed slowly, watching her march up in front of him. The gleam in his good eye grew brighter as he followed her progress, and a wry smile played round his lips. Her back was ramrod-straight, and every inch of her proclaimed her determination to come to terms with events and her reaction to them.

What a pity, he thought as she entered her bedroom without so much as a glance over her shoulder, if this deplorable situation hadn't occurred I might have made some progress on the personal front. Well, back to square one, I suppose, polite and professional until she begins to unfreeze again.

He sighed, and took himself off to bed.

# CHAPTER FIVE

To HER chagrin, Emma overslept the next morning. She was wakened by Mrs Mac bringing her a breakfast tray and the morning post.

'Oh, I can't stay in bed for breakfast!' she exclaimed in dismay. 'It's bad enough that I've slept on. Whatever will the professor think of me?'

'Och, dinna fash yoursel', it was the master who ordered your breakfast in bed. You worked right hard last night to save that lassie. Now, ye chust stay there a wee while and eat.'

Mrs Mac bustled from the room before Emma could protest further. 'I suppose everyone thinks me a weak Sassenach,' she muttered to herself half seriously, half mockingly. The knowledge that James had suggested that she have breakfast in bed was comforting, if he had done it out of concern, and not to underline her weakness. It revealed the softer, gentler side of his character that Philippa had said existed. She herself had witnessed something of this last night, both in his dealings with the girl and later when he had massaged the knots out of her neck, and the fears out of her mind.

She found that she was hungry for her tea, boiled egg, toast and marmalade. Such marmalade, she thought—another of Mrs Mac's home-made efforts, laced with enough brandy to almost give one a hangover at nine in the morning.

Having the post to deal with made her feel a little

less indolent. There was the usual mixture of professional post, letters from doctors and societies all over the world asking for the professor's advice and opinion. Some letters were from hospitals where he had worked on his recent tour, advising him of the progress being made by patients he had treated. These Emma put aside to join the ever-growing volume of information for his book.

She turned to the rest of the post, some of it junk mail asking him to join various groups and societies, or enter competitions that would win him thousands. Some were begging for a contribution to this or that worthy cause. The competitions she dumped, on his previous instructions, into the waste-paper basket, together with the literature asking him to join something. The requests for funds she put in a pile on its own. He always decided about these himself, and she'd found him very generous with his cheques to the Multiple Sclerosis Society and others.

There were two obviously personal letters in handwritten envelopes. She hated opening them, but the professor had told her that she must, as, even with his sight improving in one eye, he still had difficulty with reading.

The first letter was from an old friend in New Zealand, who had only just learned, through the stretched resources of the grapevine to that remote country, of his accident. It was a warm and affectionate letter from someone called Bob, who had been at medical school with James many years ago. Clearly they had kept in touch with each other, and the tone of the letter implied that the professor, as well as the writer, enjoyed their continued, if irregular, correspondence.

Another instance, thought Emma, of a friend as well as a colleague who valued the connection.

She opened the second personal letter.

My darling James,

I shall be bringing the children over next week for their usual stay. A little earlier than usual, but there is a reason for that, which I will explain when I see you. Both Angus and Philippa have said that I shouldn't insist on you having young James and Bess this summer, as you apparently haven't been well. I don't know what's wrong with you—you have always been such a healthy brute, ready for absolutely *anything*. Need I say more? And you only have the. . .

The bold female handwriting filled the page with the long paragraph. Emma felt sick with embarrassment. She stuffed page one and the two others that made up the whole letter back into the envelope. This, she decided, was one for James to decipher, even with his limited vision. He certainly wouldn't appreciate her reading anything so intimate.

She went off to shower and prepare herself for a late-morning start. Try as she might, she couldn't wipe out the words in the letter, written so confidently on pale blue, faintly perfumed paper.

She told herself that it was nothing to do with her what connections her employer might have; but a niggling voice kept asking why she hadn't known of this particular writer. Surely the professor or his family might have anticipated that this person would ignore the rule about phoning when there was anything personal to convey? What came over most clearly in the

letter was the writer's wilfulness, her indifference to
other people's feelings.

She was splitting hairs, of course. His private life
might be so private that even his family had no
knowledge of it. Why should they? He was obviously a
law unto himself and wouldn't necessarily feel obliged
to put his family in the picture about all his liaisons,
still less his temporary nurse cum secretary

No, that wouldn't wash, the voice in her head told
her. This writer and the children, James and Bess,
were obviously well known to the family. They stayed
at the Old House on Skye every year. Not only the
family, but Mrs Mac and the other staff, and the
neighbours and the MacLeods, must all know about
them.

She tried to rationalise her thoughts against the scant
facts that she had. Of course, the reason she hadn't
been informed by any of the MacDonalds about the
writer was that this particular visitor and her offspring
had been warned off this year. Therefore, why should
they pass on irrelevant information about this particular family connection? Clearly they hadn't expected
her to contact James by letter, and equally clearly they
had only casual or infrequent correspondence with her.

Emma gathered her tattered courage and went
downstairs to the study. To her immense relief, the
professor wasn't there, providing her with a little
respite. But not for long. She had just set the post out
in neat piles on her desk, all, that was, except the very
personal one which she was about to place on his side-
table, when he called to her from the terrace.

'Emma, arisen at last from your slumbers. How do
you feel?' and without waiting for an answer, 'Bring

the post out here; it's a beautiful morning, and I've something very interesting to tell you about last night.'

Well, at least he was in a good mood, which might put off the moment of truth for a bit. She felt very uneasy, as much for his sake as for herself, she discovered with surprise. How would he react to this letter and the intention of the writer to bring the children? Whose children? she asked herself, without really wanting to know the answer, which seemed all too obvious.

She walked out on to the terrace. James was standing, leaning on the balustrade, looking out over the bay. The white streak in his hair was as clear as a ribbon against the matt black of his thick head of hair. For all the world it looked as if he could see for miles. He couldn't, of course. As per Sir Hugh's instructions, he was still wearing his dark glasses, protecting both eyes at the beginning of the day. Later he would exchange these for one darkened lens and one thick but transparent lens, after Emma had bathed his eyes and instilled the appropriate drops.

'Shall I do your treatment now, Professor?' she asked, seeing this as a further delay before he inspected his post.

'No, I want to give you my news, and then do the post before you get to work on me.' His voice was firm and would brook no argument.

'Of course,' she replied, sounding suitably acquiescent. 'Whatever you wish.'

He looked towards her suspiciously. 'You're not going to insist on treatment first?' he asked.

'Of course not. As long as it gets done by mid-morning, a half-hour or so isn't going to make any difference.'

The professor seemed surprised. 'I thought old Toby Reid was hot on keeping to time with treatments, to deal with this wretched ME thing?'

'Dr Reid is concerned that rest, diet, treatment and exercise are spaced out properly, and that your rest and exercise periods are changed by a few minutes each day.' She looked at him closely. Was he being deliberately obtuse? Was he having her on? 'But you know that, Professor,' she said sharply. 'The doctor made it quite plain when he sent your recovery plan sheet.'

'Sorry, Nurse,' said the professor, looking anything but sorry. He grinned. 'You do rise to the bait, you know, Miss Emma Seymour.'

He was in a highly excited mood—the sort of emotional condition that nannies the world over would exclaim over and prophesy, 'Tears before bedtime.' It was so unlike the professor she was used to that she was almost alarmed. He seemed boyish, intent on casting off his mature and authoritative role. Well, the very personal letter would put a stop to all that, she felt sure.

She wished with all her heart that it hadn't arrived. There was no doubt that it spelled trouble. He should, she thought vehemently, have been allowed a little respite between all his problems.

Her anger at not being informed about the writer, or the mysterious 'children' who were mentioned, subsided, and anger on his behalf took its place. From all the evidence of his studies and research, and the operations he had performed on his recent journey, she knew that he was a dedicated surgeon. Surely he could be left alone to recover from the bug that he had picked up on his travels? A bug that he would never have contracted had he not given himself unsparingly to the poor and sick of the Third World.

Knowing how readily and accurately he could divulge her thoughts, she said quickly, 'You had something to tell me about last night?'

'Yes, Mary Maguire was here a short while ago—she thought we'd like to know the outcome of events.'

'Well, what happened, Professor? Did they find out who attacked Julie Chance?'

'Oh, yes. It was the boyfriend she was holidaying with. In fact, he presented himself at the police station in a state of terror and intoxication.'

'Oh, I am glad he gave himself up. That must mean that he cares for her, don't you think, in spite of what he did?'

'Probably. She certainly seems to care for him enough, anyway, to protect him by giving a false description of the man who was supposed to have raped her.'

'Thank goodness her boyfriend showed up! The police might have spent a long time looking for the fictitious suspect.'

'No, they wouldn't.' The professor's voice for a moment sounded grim. 'She described Hector MacLeod, down to his cravat, as the man who attacked her.'

'Dr MacLeod?' asked Emma in a horrified voice.

'Yes, poor old Hector. Just imagine the mischief she might have caused had he not been so well-known and easily able to prove that he was miles away when the rape occurred.'

'But why—why the doctor?'

'He was someone she'd seen about, easily describable, but, of course, being only a visitor here, she didn't know who he was. She was protecting her boyfriend and identified the first person who came into her head.'

'Oh, how awful! Poor Dr MacLeod. He must have been very angry.'

'From what Mary said, I think he was more sad than angry. He's a remarkable man, Emma, and a first-rate doctor. It seems that he understood the girl's motives very well, and is doing all he can to support her and her boyfriend.'

'What an amazing outcome from the night's events.'

'Indeed. By the way, Mary wanted me to confirm that your prompt action prevented Julie having a miscarriage. And the girl herself sends her thanks, as well she might. Everyone owes you a debt of gratitude, Emma.'

Emma blushed and mumbled, 'I was only doing my job.' It wasn't, she knew, because the police surgeon or Julie had praised her, but because James had passed on the message and added to it his own appreciation of her efforts.

Sensing her embarrassment, he said briskly, 'Now, let's have the post or we'll never get anything done this morning.'

He sat himself down in one of the cane chairs on the terrace, and turned his face towards her. They went though the professional mail and then the begging letters.

'Oh, good,' said the professor as they dealt with the last, stretching his tall, lean frame and making to rise.

'There are two personal letters,' said Emma quickly. 'One of them is from a doctor friend of yours named Bob, in New Zealand. Shall I read it, or will you try later?'

'I can't think of anything Bob Channing might write

that would be damning,' he grinned, 'or embarrassing
to your delicate ears, and presumably you have
skimmed through it?'

'Yes.'

'OK, let's have it, then.'

It was, as Emma had already gathered, an amusing,
long, chatty letter, commiserating with James over his
injury and illness and wishing him well, then going on
to recall past times and some of their youthful esca-
pades. He was the sort of person who wrote as he
probably spoke, almost without drawing breath, in
long sentences. The letter ended with an open invita-
tion, obviously being repeated, for James to visit and
stay with him and Becky.

'His wife,' interjected James. 'Lovely girl.'

Emma paused briefly, and continued,

'. . .who is dying to see you again. She wants to
know if you still fancy her! Come to that, I'd like to
know if you still fancy me. Joke, James! It's been a
hell of a long time since we went on a bender
together. About time we did something about it. If
you can't get to good old New Zealand, and we can't
get to your precious island, perhaps we can meet
halfway. Give it some thought. Singapore perhaps,
or Hong Kong, before it becomes part of the Chinese
empire.'

It astonished Emma how casually some people spoke
of travelling from one end of the globe to the other.
The professor, for instance, on one of his work tapes
had announced nonchalantly that he was off to Sri
Lanka the following day. At the time he had mentioned
it he had been scrubbing up for surgery in Athens!

He astonished her again now by saying, 'Well, what

about that, then, Emma—would you like to see something of the Orient before it changes out of all recognition? We might plan a little jaunt in a few weeks' time, when I'm done with these.' He waved an eloquent hand at his dark glasses.

Emma was speechless for a moment, both at his suggestion and because for the first time he had referred to his eye condition as if he believed that it might heal. Her delight at his first expressed positive reaction to the future thrilled her.

She swallowed and replied huskily, 'You won't need me when you've dispensed with those, Professor.'

'Need, Emma?' He looked towards her as if he could see her plainly, staring hard. 'Needs come in all shapes and disguises, don't you think? Anyway,' he introduced a plaintive note into his voice, 'what about this ME thing? That may not be cleared up by then, and I'm sure Toby Reid wouldn't want me to return to a full working schedule until I was over that particular hurdle.' He smiled to show that he was half jesting while at the same time expecting her to give serious consideration to what he had said.

She didn't know what to make of him in this mood. She was perhaps more uncertain how to respond because she was aware of holding a bomb in her hand, in the shape of the second personal letter that had arrived in the post that morning.

Her reply was consequently cool and considered.

'Well, I'm sure that your Dr Reid, Dr MacLeod and Sir Hugh will be the best judges of your fitness to work or travel, Professor.'

'Emma, you're priceless,' James said with a laugh. 'Now, is there anything more?'

She was about to hand him the second letter and

explain to the best of her ability why she couldn't read it, when there was a shriek from inside the house. Following hot on the shriek came Oona, the girl who helped Mrs Mac with the domestic chores. She burst on to the terrace and in a frightened voice, almost a whisper, and to Emma's ears incomprehensible, as it was in Gaelic, poured out a long explanation to James.

He rose from his chair, said something to the girl in Gaelic, and then spoke to Emma.

'Sorry about the language,' he apologised. 'Oona, as you've probably guessed, is rather upset. It appears that MacPhearson the gardener has put a fork through his foot.'

'Well, we'd better have a look at it,' said Emma.

The professor was making his way to the french windows, following the agitated Oona. He stopped long enough to let out a bellow of laughter, and comment, still laughing. 'What an advertisement you are, Emma, to the nursing profession and your old training hospital. Totally cool and collected in the face of an emergency.'

'If it is an emergency, Professor, we should get there as fast as we can.'

'He's not bleeding profusely, or in shock, Emma, I've elicited from Oona. Mrs Mac sent her for our help, but I gather the incident occurred a while ago.'

'But she yelled.' Emma slowed down behind him. 'I thought he was haemorrhaging to death!'

'Young women sometimes tend to be a bit dramatic.'

'So it's not true, then, about a fork through the man's foot?' She hung back in the doorway leading from the terrace. 'You won't need me.'

'We need you, my dear—I'm still blind as the proverbial bat, and he must have attention. Oh, yes, it's true enough, but he's done things like this before. He probably wouldn't have said anything, but Mrs Mac saw what happened and insisted on reporting it.'

'But tetanus. . .other infections. . .the pain?'

'I give all my staff inti-tet injections regularly. Most of them think it's a joke, especially Auld Mac. As to anything else, I should think that he's immune to practically everything he can pick up from the soil; must have immunised himself a dozen times over. But he'll need the wound looked at and possibly need to go over to Casualty, if only for form's sake.'

Auld Mac was sitting in Mrs Mac's kitchen, drinking tea and scoffing fruit cake. He made to rise as Emma and the professor followed Oona into the room.

The professor said something to him in Gaelic, and the old man responded with a chuckling reply and a near-toothless grin. He pointed to his enormous wellington boots and the hole in one of them at instep level, and then, apparently remembering that the professor couldn't see where he was pointing, he grabbed his hand and placed it over the gaping hole from which was oozing sticky dark blood.

To Emma's surprise, the professor seemed undisturbed by this pantomime.

'Hmm,' he said softly, and turned towards where he knew Emma was standing. 'The wound's about the size of my finger. Of course, the silly old fool has made it worse by wiggling the prong in order to get it out.' In spite of his words, James smiled affectionately and patted the gardener's hand.

'Oh, no.' Emma stood beside MacPhearson and gave him a reassuring smile, though she guessed that it was wasted on the tough old man. 'We'll have to have your boot off,' she said, though she didn't think he would understand.

She bent to take hold of the boot, but Mrs Mac intervened.

'Chust you let Oona do that, miss. You wait awhile and tend the silly auld man's foot when it's exposed like.' Clearly there was a distinction between nursing chores and others as far as Mrs Mac was concerned.

The professor grinned.

'I should do as Mrs Mac says, Emma,' he said. 'I always do.'

It was astonishing to her that everyone, including the gardener, who she thought must be in considerable pain, should treat the matter as a joke. Even Oona, who had been properly shaken at the outset, seemed to be taking things in her stride, though she did jump back with a little cry of surprise when she pulled off the boot and a mess of dirty bloody sock came to light.

The wound was filled with debris. Strands of wool from the thick, unwashed socks had embedded themselves into the cavity the prong of the fork had produced. There was also soil and sand from the garden, and a twist of what looked like leaves of some kind.

Emma commented on these to the professor, and he asked MacPhearson to explain them.

'Apparently,' James told Emma, 'he treated the wound with an old herbal recipe, snake root bound up in blackcurrant leaves. He made it into a plug and stuffed it into the cavity.'

'I'll have to wash out the debris,' Emma said to the professor. 'Perhaps a saline solution would be suitable, and I'll remove the plug with forceps. Will you explain to him, please?'

'Oh, he understands you well enough, don't you, Mac?' The old man continued to grin toothlessly.

Emma shrugged and explained what she was going to do to his foot. He seemed not the least perturbed, just grinned and nodded and went on munching his cake.

Cleaning the wound turned out to be a formidable job. What with the home-made dressing of leaves and roots, the recently acquired rubbish from his socks and his digging, and the almost certain unwashed state of his feet prior to the accident, it took Emma a considerable time to cleanse it to her satisfaction.

'What does it need, Emma?' asked the professor when she had finished. 'A stitch or two, or would surface butterflies do the job?'

'I'd like to pack it with a dressing after drenching it with cicatrin powder, and send him over to the hospital for their opinion. I think he should have stitches, as it's quite clear that he'll carry on working with it, so butterflies might not be strong enough.'

'Right, we'll take him over in the Range Rover, Emma. A little jaunt will do us both good. Look, you do what's necessary here and I'll give Casualty at Kilbeg a ring to let them know that we're coming.'

James went on to explain to MacPhearson what was going to happen, addressing him as 'Auld Mac', which Emma could just decipher from the Gaelic.

'I thought you said that he understands English though he doesn't speak it?' she said rather peevishly.

The professor looked crestfallen.

'I thought it would be kinder coming to him in his mother tongue,' he said. 'Besides, although he understands English, I don't think he finds much comfort in it.'

Emma, ever honest, said softly, 'I'm not surprised—
the Gaelic you all speak sounds so soft and gentle.'

Everyone in the kitchen smiled their pleasure at her
words.

'Miss Emma Seymour,' said the professor, clearly
very pleased with her comment, 'what a remarkable
lady you are! Perhaps a little fey. Perhaps a little
Scottish blood courses through your veins, yes?' he
asked in a teasing, gentle voice.

Mrs Mac, seeing Emma blush and shake her head,
and knowing that the effect of his words was unseen by
the professor, spoke sharply. 'Well, the sooner you are
all away from my kitchen, the better.' She relented a
little. 'Auld Mac can stay put till the professor's made
his call and the arrangements are set for Kilbeg.'

The professor raised his hands in mock surrender.
'We're away, Mrs Mac, and will leave you in peace.'

They left the kitchen, he to make his telephone call,
Emma to the study surgery to pick up the dressings she
needed to make MacPhearson comfortable for the
journey.

James was stepping out very confidently, as he
always did in this fairly narrow corridor, running his
hand along the smooth wall for guidance.

Emma had to make a little running skip to catch up
with him.

'James, wait,' she said as she caught up with him and
laid a detaining hand on his arm. 'I must do your eye
treatment before we go. Please wait in the surgery; I
won't be long seeing to MacPhearson.'

'Must I have it done before we go? You said yourself
that it wasn't essential to the minute.'

'To the minute? You must be kidding! It's going to
be past midday if we leave it till after the hospital. Yes,

you must have it done now, Professor. I'll not drive you or MacPhearson anywhere until your treatment is done.'

'Oh, we're back to "Professor", are we?'

'But I always call you Professor.' She felt herself blushing and was glad he couldn't see her. Why did the least personal comment from him seem heavy with meaning? She hadn't realised she had just addressed him as James. His Christian name seemed to spring unnoticed to her lips when she was under any excitement or stress.

Since she was standing close to him in the confines of the corridor, he had no difficulty in locating her hands, which he captured and held between his.

'Dear Nurse Emma Seymour,' he said in the dry, laughing tone he used when saying her whole name, 'I'm quite literally in your beautiful hands.' He raised them to his lips and kissed each finger slowly and deliberately.

Emma snatched her hands away and stepped past him.

'I mean it,' she said, trying to make her voice sound firm and untroubled by the touch of his lips. 'Your treatment before I go anywhere.'

The professor gave a quiet chuckle.

'So be it,' he said softly. 'I'll do as I'm bid and wait in the surgery after I've phoned Kilbeg.'

The journey to the hospital was uneventful. The rough road was almost deserted, and Emma was becoming used to its bends and twists, and the half-mile of sheer cliff on one side and the drop to the shore on the other.

At the hospital they were given VIP treatment.

Obviously the professor was much respected, both as a medical person of note and the local bigwig.

Emma's work on the wound was praised, an attitude that seemed to give the professor much pleasure. Auld Mac was Gaelicly garrulous, casting sly glances at Emma as he recounted his version of the accident and treatment.

The casualty registrar told them that Julie Chance and her boyfriend had both been moved to Portree.

'You did a good job on that poor girl too, Miss Seymour,' he said. 'She was most grateful to you for your efforts.'

Emma found that she was rather embarrassed by all this praise. Surely she had only done what was required of her as a nurse? She said as much to the professor as they drove home, with MacPhearson comfortably ensconced on the back seat, and James sitting beside her.

'You must appreciate,' explained James, 'that until recently, and with the opening up of the island to campers and caravanners, the more unpleasant crimes of the mainland had not been visited upon us. Rape,' he added drily, 'being one of them.'

The rest of the journey was completed in silence, with James apparently deep in thought and Emma concentrating on driving over the rough terrain at the tail end of their journey. MacPhearson was apparently enjoying his own kind of Gaelic dream.

It was not until she was getting ready for bed that night that Emma remembered the second personal letter for the professor. She hadn't noticed it in the pocket of her cardigan when she'd showered and changed for dinner. Evidently the professor too had forgotten that she'd mentioned a second letter. For a moment, already in her nightclothes, Emma wondered if she should take it to him. He might still be on the terrace, bracing the smudgies while enjoying the brief twilight of a northern night.

A still, small voice persuaded her to leave it till the morning. He'd had enough for one day. Let him enjoy a peaceful night, undisturbed by responsibilities from the past. Another few hours would make no difference.

She was tired, but couldn't get to sleep at once.

What had the professor been thinking about, she wondered, on their silent trip back from the hospital with Auld Mac? Had he been regretting his words and actions that morning when he had teased her about using his Christian name? Perhaps he regretted kissing her fingers in such a delicate, gentle manner, when he'd trapped her in the corridor?

Had he been put off by her quick reaction to his advances? Was he in fact making advances? She could never be sure with him. His way of life seemed so far from her own that it might be just a polite way of saying thank you in the circles in which he must normally move. The society women he was at home with would probably have accepted his gesture without turning a hair.

And yet the way he looked at her sometimes with his one good eye, the way he had of sometimes dropping his voice to a husky drawl when he spoke to her, the way that night he had stood at the foot of the stairs and murmured her name, surely this was meant just for her? Surely he was trying to tell her something of his true feelings, without shedding all his reserve, his professional reticence? If only she was capable of breaking through the barrier of her own fear of being rejected. If only she could believe that a man like James could be in love with her!

She sighed, switched off the light, and settled down to sleep.

James, on the terrace beneath her window, wearing his one blind lens and one cloudy but light-enhancing lens, saw her light go out.

He heaved himself out of the chair, switched off the lights, and made his way upstairs to his room.

# CHAPTER SIX

EMMA woke early after a good night's sleep. Her first thought was of the letter, and her tummy churned in anticipation of the professor's reaction when she presented him with it. Reviewing the little she had read of the missive, it seemed somehow more sinister, more threatening in retrospect.

She was down to the breakfast table before him and had sorted the day's post before he put in an appearance. There was nothing personal today, she noted with relief, and cravenly decided that she would still further delay yesterday's letter until after breakfast.

'Morning,' she said brightly when James entered. 'Did you sleep well, Professor?'

'Yes, thank you; and you, Emma?'

Emma confirmed that she had. It was their usual exchange at the breakfast table.

'Not a lot of post this morning,' she said, trying to sound casual. She put out a hand to the three letters from hospitals where he had recently been working. They were all progress reports, and all favourable. That, she felt, was a good omen. 'Shall I start with the hospital letters?'

The professor spoke in a deep, velvet-soft voice, and an altogether too innocent expression on his face.

'Perhaps yesterday's letter that we didn't get around to.' He paused. Emma swallowed, her mouth dry. 'You did say that there was a second personal letter, did you not?'

Emma nodded. Even she sometimes forgot that he couldn't see such small physical movements. Remembering, she found her tongue.

'Yes, of course—the other personal letter. Well, Professor, I just started reading it, but I think that you should try to decipher it for yourself. Here.' She pulled the envelope from her pocket and thrust it towards him, tapping the back of his hand with the paper so that he should know that it was available.

He ignored the letter.

'Why won't you read it to me, Emma?' he asked. 'You read Bob's letter, and I'm quite happy for you to be involved with my personal affairs. In fact,' he looked up from his plate at which he had been peering, 'I have no wish to have any secrets from you, my dear, none at all.'

'I'm sorry, Professor, I just can't read it, and I'm sure when you see it you would prefer me not to have read it.'

The expression on the professor's face changed, hardened, became more lined, more austere. He obviously realised from her tone that this was something unpleasant, surprising. It must have given him a clue as to the writer's identity.

He asked harshly, 'What's the address it's sent from?'

'The Rue du Jardin des Olives.'

The professor snatched the letter hovering between them from her hand.

'Right, I'll deal with this.' He scraped his chair back from the table, and stood up. He was very angry, but made an effort to control his anger. 'Give me half an hour, Emma, then you can come and do my treatment, and later we'll attend to this morning's post.' He started across the room. 'Why don't you go for a walk or something? It'll do you good.'

He obviously wanted her out of the house. She heard him go to the study, and minutes later the receiver in the dining-room clicked briefly as he picked up the phone in the other room.

She let herself out through the french windows on to the terrace and down the path to the shore. It was hard not to think of the opening words of the letter and wonder what the professor had made of them, and what the rest of the letter said. She was warmed by the memory of his firm words telling her that he wanted no secrets from her. Only when he'd known the identity of that particular writer had the shutters come down.

The beach was deserted as usual at that time of the morning. It was ten o'clock or so before the campers from the field over the cliff were about. The bay, she had learned from Mrs Mac, belonged to the MacDonalds and the Old House, but the professor made no attempt to keep the campers out. For their part, they were probably unaware of the fact that they were trespassing whenever they played or picnicked on the sand.

It was another golden day. Emma took off her sandals and walked barefooted along the beach. She enjoyed the sensation of the warm sand trickling between her toes, but she couldn't get the professor, or the letter and its contents, such as she had read, out of her mind.

The writer was obviously closely associated with James. A nasty niggling feeling that she had been even closer in the past worried away at the back of Emma's mind. The children had been mentioned casually and familiarly. 'I shall be bringing the children. . .earlier than usual,' the letter had stated.

And the boy was called James; Emma rolled the fact round in her head. So what? A common enough name, especially here in Scotland. Why should there be any more significance in it than that? Perhaps they were distant members of the family, cousins, or second cousins. The professor had told her one evening when they were taking their stroll here along the bay that the MacDonalds were both a large family and a large clan.

'Although we're scattered all over the world,' he'd said, 'we're very close. We have a gathering every few years, and hundreds turn up from everywhere.' He had grinned in the beguiling way he had. 'Some of us,' he had said, 'are quite black, you know. The Scots, of course, are great ones for travelling and taking their genes, as well as their expertise, to far-away places.'

It had been a magical night, as so many had been since Emma had arrived on Skye, and she hadn't been sure that he wasn't making fun of her. Sensing, as he so often did, her thoughts, he'd confirmed, 'It's true, my dear, every word of it.'

So perhaps, she thought, making her way back along the beach, this is just part of the far-flung family or clan. Maybe the writer is simply someone who is used to bringing her children here to this lovely island for a few weeks each summer. She just happens to be a selfish, inconsiderate bitch, who disregarded Philippa's and Angus's word about the professor's condition, and is dumping them on him anyway. At least the writer didn't mention staying; that was some comfort anyway.

A small voice inside her head warned her not to rejoice over something that she knew little about.

Another voice asked why it was important that the writer was not to be resident at the Old House.

She didn't really want to ask this question of herself; it was better left unacknowledged. Of course, in all truth she could tell herself that the professor needed a regular regime to restore him to health, and plenty of time to get on with his book. Both strong reasons for Emma, as his nurse and secretary, to resent intruders.

It was the truth, but only half the truth. To be honest, she didn't want anyone intruding on the intimate and quiet lifestyle that she and the professor had fallen into. A pattern of calm contentment filled her days and, until this morning, she thought, had filled the professor's likewise.

The various outside interruptions, like the rape, MacPhearson's injury, and the entertaining of the MacLeods a week or so back and their reciprocal visit, only seemed to underline their growing satisfaction in each other's company.

Of course, Emma admitted, sitting on a sun-warmed rock and dabbling her feet in the water, it was possible that James was not as content as she; but nothing in his demeanour even hinted at his wanting things to change. In fact, quite the reverse, ever since the dinner party at the MacLeods'.

In spite of his continuing need of her as his 'eyes' for much of the time, he managed to convey strength and protection. In the areas of the house and garden with which he was totally familiar, he tended to put a hand under her elbow when they were walking side by side. There had been one night, the night that they had dined with the MacLeods, when he had kissed her again—only a gentle kiss as they had entered the hall, and she had stood at the bottom of the stairs to wish him goodnight. It had seemed very natural for him to cross the hall, take her face in his hands and brush her lips with his.

'Goodnight, dear girl,' he had said softly. 'It was a wonderful evening, thanks to you and my old friends. I feel that I'm beginning to make strides forward at last. My thanks, Emma, you dear, dear girl.'

Sleep hadn't come easily that night, but she had found that it wasn't unpleasant lying awake and reliving the evening, and most of all James's goodnight kiss. It had rounded off a very pleasant evening in the MacLeods' comfortable old-fashioned house in the nearby town.

The food had been plain but good, and Maggie at her anecdotal best when relaying stories of the good, bad old days in the nursing profession. But it had been the presence of the professor, oozing a strong, calm masculinity, that had made her evening. By accident or design, he had managed to touch her on several occasions, making her heart thump and her cheeks grow rosy and warm.

Extraordinary, but she had been sure that he had known how she was responding to his touch in spite of his blindness, whereas the MacLeods, hopefully, had been blissfully unaware of what was happening.

She had wondered if there would be any restraint or signs of regret in his manner when they met the next morning, but he had been as usual. They had greeted each other with a customary enquiry about how each had slept, and passed on to the post.

Well, the letter he'd been landed with this morning had shattered all that. The fact that it had ever been sent had spoiled the harmony that had been growing between them. He had quite definitely shut her out;

made it plain that neither her presence or opinion was
wanted where this particular problem was concerned.
All this in spite of his having said that he wanted no
secrets from her. Obviously this was one secret that
hadn't been included in his generous suggestion.

Emma looked at her watch and saw that the half-
hour he had stipulated was nearly up. She walked back
along the hot sand, carrying her sandals. As she
approached the house she saw that the professor was
standing on the terrace in his favourite position, leaning
on the balustrade, looking straight out across the bay
to where the Cuillins rose majestically from the
peninsula.

Though she made no sound in her bare feet, he
sensed that she was coming.

'Well,' he called casually as she started up the garden
path, 'I'm ready and waiting for my treatment.'

Emma tried to adopt the same throwaway attitude.

'I've been half an hour, Professor, to the dot,' she
replied with a little laugh.

She joined him on the terrace and they turned
together to go through to the study and the little
surgery.

'Emma. . .' he laid a hand on her bare arm '. . .you
must have read the first page of this letter,' he touched
his pocket, 'so you know something about a visit being
planned. I'm trying to stop this happening. It'll mess
up our work and treatment schedule, and that can't be
allowed to happen, can it?'

'No, no, of course not,' murmured Emma uncer-
tainly, not knowing what he expected of her. She had
rather thought that he might keep silent about the
letter, but it was as if he was trying to make light of
something that was in fact no light matter.

He wasn't the sort of man to prevaricate, and yet that was precisely what he seemed to be doing. It was true what he had said about visitors interfering with both his work and his treatment, but she was positive that he had other reasons for not wanting these particular visitors.

He still had his hand on her arm. He tightened his grip and marched rather than guided her across the study.

He almost unnerved her by saying softly, 'Your skin is beautifully warm, Emma. I bet you're getting a very fetching tan. We must do as much work as possible outside on the terrace today, make the most of the sunshine. The weathermen are forecasting a change by the end of the week.'

She didn't know how to respond to this comment, which was surely a compliment. Clearly he had no intention of continuing the conversation about unwelcome visitors. Emma was rather relieved. If he wasn't going to be entirely open with her she would rather he ignored the matter; it might help her to put it and the unknown writer out of her mind.

'We'd better press on with your treatment, Professor,' she said, trying to sound professional but to her own ears sounding prim.

The professor sat himself in the surgical chair and leaned back. Emma took up her position behind his head and began to remove the dressings. She knew before she had finished uncovering his 'good' eye that something was wrong. The pad was soiled and she had difficulty, even with saline swabs, easing it from his lids.

'Trouble?' asked the professor calmly, aware of the care she was taking to remove the pad.

'Rather more sticky than usual, Professor, that's all.'

'Hmm, a fungal infection, do you think?'

Emma could have wept when she exposed the eye completely. It looked worse than the first time she had seen it, red and puffy and oozing an unpleasant discharge. 'Well!' she said, reluctant to commit herself.

The professor wrinkled his fine patrician nose. 'I'm afraid it is, Emma,' he said quietly. 'I've smelt that particular odour too often before on patients.'

All her instincts shouted at her to sound reassuring and dispute his own immediate diagnosis, but she couldn't do that to him. He deserved her honesty. She too had seen and smelt conditions like this; all fungal infections tended to produce this unpleasant odour.

'I'm going to irrigate this eye, James, and put a clean dressing over it. I'll then finish your other treatment and afterwards phone Dr MacLeod and ask him to call.'

She had half expected an argument from the professor, but instead received a wry smile and a surprising comment.

'What a pity that only an aurora borealis or an emergency can prevail upon you to use my Christian name, Emma. Perhaps you might try to use it more often and so not tempt the gods, yes?'

He was, of course, being terribly brave. Of all people, he had to be aware of the dangers of a fresh infection, his lowered resistance to it, and the awful possibility of his other eye becoming affected.

'I'll try,' she whispered, and then got on with the job she was trained for, irrigating, swabbing, changing dressings with the best non-touch technique that she could muster.

She left the professor drinking coffee while she phoned Dr MacLeod.

He had already left the surgery, but Janet, his receptionist, promised to try to track him down on his rounds. The doctor rang in some fifteen minutes later when Emma was having her own coffee, sitting opposite the professor on the terrace.

Emma gave the GP all the information she could about the infection and filled him in as to what she had done.

'Right, I'll be with you in about half an hour,' said Hector MacLeod. 'You've done all you can, Emma; now don't go fretting yourself. Even the treatment is a risk with James's condition. You know that and would accept it if it were anyone else.'

Emma pondered over this remark later, and Hector's powers of perception. Was she more concerned because James was a distinguished member of the medical profession, or because he was simply James? In the short while that she had been on Skye they had become close, because they worked together, but she mustn't let herself believe there was more to it than that—even if she felt a tremor every time he touched her, or blushed at his mildest compliments. A few hours before she had longed to believe that there might be something brewing between them. Now she wavered yet again.

He was simply an extraordinary employer, with a razor-sharp intelligence allied to a gentle manner where patients, or those less fortunate, were concerned. She recalled what his brother and sister had said about him not suffering fools gladly. This was true with those he expected to reach certain standards, with his colleagues and equals. But this wasn't the whole picture. She had

seen enough of him in action on video, working in
Theatre or talking to nervous patients, and in the flesh,
behaving with tenderness and care to the rape victim
and Auld Mac, to know that impatience with ineptitude
was only one facet of his nature.

They spent the half-hour between Hector's phone
call and his arrival going through the day's post. Emma
found it shattering, trying to carry on as if nothing had
happened when perhaps her worst fears, and, what was
more pertinent, James's worst fears, might be realised,
and he would become completely blind.

James seemed able to set aside his fears and concentrate on the matter in hand. She made herself do the
same, but they were both relieved when Hector's voice
was heard in the hall as Mrs Mac opened the front
door.

They heard him refusing coffee at that moment, but
confirming that he would have some later after he'd
examined Master Jamie.

In spite of her anxiety, Emma found a moment to
think how touching it was that the doctor and housekeeper so often fell into the habit of speaking of James
in this affectionate manner. This only seemed to
happen when they were in conversation together, as if
they were constantly reminded of the role he had been
forced to play when his father had died and he was still
little more than a child. Too young to be called master
proper, or even mister, but elevated from just the boy
Jamie.

'Well,' said the doctor as he walked on to the terrace,
'here's a sad thing to have happened, James. A fungal
infection, so Emma tells me. We'd better have a look.
Let's go through to the treatment-room.'

For some reason his attitude surprised Emma. She

had thought he might approach the matter more obliquely, perhaps allowing that there might be an error in diagnosis. After all, he only had her telephone explanation of the problem. As a nurse, she might be wrong in her assumption; there were many conditions that might take on the appearance of a particular kind of infection and perhaps be due to another cause.

The doctor caught her eye. He had clearly read her thoughts. Am I so transparent, she wondered, or is it this Celtic perception to see beyond the obvious, to reach out and feel one's ideas and emotions? She had almost got used to the professor's ability to do this, but had never been sure whether this was something just between the two of them, or part of a national characteristic.

'Your word is good enough for me, Emma,' the doctor explained as they preceded James to the study. 'And I don't doubt that our friend here——' he jerked his head backwards to indicate the professor '—added his opinion to yours.'

'Yes, we're both agreed that it is a fungal infection.'

'Then let's see what can be done about it,' said Dr MacLeod in his soft, reassuring Highland tones.

For the first time that morning since uncovering the professor's eye Emma felt some hope. If anyone could do or suggest anything that might be done it was this sturdy Scottish GP who had known and loved James since he was a boy.

The professor sat down once again in the surgical chair, and Emma removed the freshly soiled dressing from his eye.

A quick look at the exudate on the gauze pad told Dr MacLeod all he needed to know, but he spent some time examining his friend's eye.

'May I use your phone, James?' he asked after the examination. 'I want to ring Sir Hugh, put him in the picture, and see what he suggests.'

'You must do what you must, Hector,' replied the professor in resigned tones. 'His number's there on the pad.'

'I should like to phone from the study, James, if that's all right with you.'

'As you wish.'

Dr MacLeod left the treatment-room. Emma placed a clean dressing over the affected eye.

'Can I do anything for you, James, while we wait for Hector?'

'Just be here, my dear, and remember to call me James.' He put out a hand and squeezed hers, for once fluttering uselessly over the dressings tray. 'You know, Hugh Robertson and Hector will come up with something between them, and you'll perform your usual miracles in carrying out their treatment.'

'Oh, James!' She was unable to control the tears that suddenly streamed down her cheeks. 'I should be comforting you, not you trying to cheer me up. What a hell of a nurse I'm turning out to be!' She sniffed and fumbled for her handkerchief with the one hand he had released, but couldn't prevent a huge tear-drop falling on his wrist.

'Emma,' he whispered in a surprised voice, 'do you care so much?'

'Surely you know I do!'

It was difficult to tell who was the most surprised: Emma, because she thought that he had guessed how she felt—he always seemed to know everything, and she was sure she had given herself away on several occasions—or James, because he had suppressed his feelings, refusing to acknowledge them as being more than an interest in a pretty woman under frustrating circumstances, almost since she had arrived.

The moment passed. Dr MacLeod came into the room in his large, soft-footed way, and announced, 'Sir Hugh's coming this evening, flying up in his helicopter. He'll sort out about landing on the beach and so on. Meanwhile, Emma, you're to saline bathe the eye every two hours, and James, you're to have plenty of rest, no work today, and pain-killers as necessary.'

James was already looking mutinous and was obviously going to protest, when the elderly GP held up his hand and said firmly, 'If you don't co-operate, James, I'll bloody well give you a sedative injection myself. Come on, be sensible, man. It's not fair to any of us who are trying to get you back to full health to jeopardise the situation further.'

'Please, James?' asked Emma softly.

The professor swallowed his anger and disappointment. 'OK, I'll toe the line.'

Dr MacLeod stayed for a while, drinking his coffee and steadily eating his way through a mountain of Mrs Mac's drop scones.

Emma escorted him out at last.

'Now, don't forget, lass, any problems, any at all,' he emphasised, 'let me know at once. I'll leave a list of numbers for Janet, so that she can get hold of me in a trice. I'll never be more than half an hour away.'

He packed himself into his ancient jeep and took off at a leap, spurting up the gravel, and raising a hand in farewell as he swept round the drive and out of the gates.

Emma was both glad and sorry to see him go. While he had been there on the spot she had felt comforted by his medical presence. Never had she been so unsure of herself nursing-wise. She knew that it was because she had never before been so intimately involved with a patient. But one part of her rejoiced at his departure, for surely now she and James could continue to examine their feelings for each other.

She felt rather breathless at the thought. She even wondered if the broken, disjointed conversation, with all its undertones, had ever taken place between her and James, just prior to Hector's return to the treatment-room. Perhaps she had invested it with more importance than it warranted. Maybe the look on James's face and his surprised acknowledgement of her feelings weren't quite what they seemed.

Perhaps because they were both upset by Dr MacLeod's obvious concern over the eye condition they had both over-reacted.

When she returned from seeing Hector off James had moved to the terrace. He was lying back in one of the cushioned cane reclining chairs, with his feet elevated on the pull-out stool.

'There,' he said as she reached the terrace, 'how's that for obeying Doctor's and my favourite nurse's orders?'

'Amazing,' said Emma with a little laugh, trying to match his nonchalance. 'Can I get you anything?'

'No, I'll do as instructed and rest before lunch.'

She couldn't stop a small disappointed sigh escaping. 'Oh, right, I'll get on with those lecture notes from yesterday.'

'Yes, thank you, Emma, please do that,' he replied in a pleasant but cool and distant voice.

* * *

For a few minutes before she started work Emma sat motionless in front of her typewriter. She'd been given the biggest brush-off she'd ever encountered. One moment James had been all warmth and affection, the next issuing polite, meaningless instructions.

She was disgusted with herself to find tears blurring her eyes for the second time that morning. Clearly the professor had used the time between Hector's departure and her return to reconsider their emotional words of a few minutes earlier. Clearly he wished they had never happened.

Right, just as clearly her course was defined for her. If reference to the situation was ever made again she must convince him that it was simply concern for his welfare as friend and nurse that had overwhelmed her. Never must he know of the blinding sensation of love and helplessness that had enveloped her at the thought of his suffering.

He might just buy that, she thought. After all, the word 'love' had not featured in their conversation. It had not been the words they had used but their pent-up emotion that had lent them significance.

Resolutely she dried her eyes and blew her nose, and belted away at the typing up of yesterday's notes with ferocious speed and concentration.

The rest of the day was very peculiar. Mrs Mac brought them lunch on the terrace and they carried on a polite but meaningless conversation. Emma attended to the professor's eye every two hours as instructed, and resettled him comfortably on the terrace after each session. Yet, in spite of this, she felt lonelier than she had ever felt in her life. There was a massive emptiness inside her that neither hard work nor her moments with the professor could fill.

She felt cold too, though the day was as warm as the professor had promised that morning when he'd suggested that they work on the terrace. That conversation, and even his angry reception of the letter, had receded into some distant memory. The only reality was his eye infection and the dreadful possibilities that it conjured up.

Emma longed for Sir Hugh to come and prescribe something magic to take away the infection and the pain for James. For, although the professor would admit to no more than discomfort, neither she nor Dr MacLeod quite believed his brave words.

So the afternoon drifted into early evening. They had a sort of high tea, since they weren't sure of the time that Sir Hugh would arrive. Neither of them had much appetite, picking at the delicious salad and fresh fruit that Mrs Mac spread before them.

The housekeeper was a tower of strength. Hector MacLeod had given her a background picture of the problem before he had left, and she had assured Emma that she was at hand to help in whatever way needed.

The two women now exchanged glances as Mrs Mac removed the professor's almost untouched food.

'It's to be hoped that yon clever eye man arrives soon,' she said drily, touching the professor's shoulder with a gentle hand, 'or you'll be starving to death.'

For the first time that day James laughed. It was a tremendous, bellowing laugh. It was a relief to have the uncomfortable silence that had reigned between them broken.

'My dear Mrs Mac, you're a priceless bonny lass.' He smiled and found her hand and gave it a squeeze.

Mrs Mac looked pleased and finished loading up the

trolley. At that moment they all three heard the sound of an approaching aircraft.

'It's Hugh,' said James, and to Emma's sensitive ear his voice held a mixture of relief and anxiety.

They all looked towards the bay as the helicopter came into sight, circling low over the water and making for the far end of the beach.

'Go to meet him, Emma,' said the professor. 'I'll make for the treatment-room.' He cleared this throat. 'For God's sake, don't let us get bogged down in the social niceties until he's done his worst.'

It was the nearest that Emma had seen him to losing his nerve.

She made her way down the path and walked towards where the helicopter was settling in a mini-sand-storm.

'Please God,' she prayed, 'let Sir Hugh be able to help my darling James. Don't let him go blind!'

# CHAPTER SEVEN

EVEN though it was mid-evening, it was still brilliantly sunny, with thin skeins of wispy clouds draped across the Cuillins.

Emma walked along the sands as she had that very morning, but with an even heavier heart. Then she had been concerned about James because of the letter that had clearly angered him; now she came to greet the man who held her employer's whole future in the skill of his mind and hand. She would have given anything to be worrying merely about the insignificant problems of that morning.

Sir Hugh, a rotund, gnomic little man, advanced to meet her, materialising out of the swirl of sand thrown up by the rotary blades of the helicopter. She had no difficulty in identifying him, although he was accompanied by a tall, thin, rather elegant man who, in looks, better fitted the role of a distinguished consultant than Sir Hugh himself. But what Sir Hugh lacked in height, he made up for in authority. It manifested itself even at the distance of twenty feet.

He held out a hand as they approached each other, and gave Emma a charming smile.

'You are, of course, Miss Seymour, James's paragon of a nurse. Lucky James!'

They shook hands, and Emma said, 'I don't feel much like a paragon, nor even a good nurse at the moment, Sir Hugh, having let this happen.'

'My dear Miss Seymour, had you not been here the damage might have occurred earlier, and would almost certainly not have been discovered till later. And I have it from Dr MacLeod that you're meticulous in your non-touch technique, and have so far prevented the other eye from becoming infected.'

Emma nodded. The tall, thin man strode over to them, carrying several leather bags and boxes. Sir Hugh introduced him.

'Roger Foulds, my registrar.'

'Hi,' said the registrar, lifting his laden hands helplessly to show that he couldn't shake hands.

'Hello; can I help?' asked Emma.

'Oh, Roger can manage,' said Sir Hugh, taking her by the arm and marching her along the beach. 'Now, I want you to tell me everything about this eye of James's.'

Emma did so. Courteously the consultant steered her before him from the terrace into the house.

James was standing by the reclining surgical chair as they entered. He held out a hand to Sir Hugh, unerringly finding the right position and height.

'Hugh, it's very good of you to come. I hope it isn't on a wild-goose chase. You're busy enough without me adding to your problems.'

The consultant took both James's hands in his. 'We both know that this is serious, old chap. You came like a shot when Stella and I needed you. You don't think that I'd do less for you, surely?'

James realised that there was someone else in the room, and must have guessed who it was.

'Hello, Roger,' he said cheerfully, waving a hand in the general direction of the registrar.

'Hi, James,' replied Roger. 'Sorry you've got problems, but my revered boss will no doubt sort you out.'

'And how!' answered James, managing a laugh.

Sir Hugh examined James's blind eye first, before the covering was removed from the infected eye. It took him a long time, with his registrar handing him various instruments from the cases he had brought with him. Some of them Emma had never seen before.

'Sir Hugh has designed many of his own instruments,' explained Roger, 'so they're not generally available.'

Sir Hugh said to James, 'Well, this is good news, James, is it not? The damaged tissue in this eye has repaired well. The optic nerve is out of danger. There's absolutely no reason why this eye shouldn't continue to improve without any impairment of sight. That's something, old chap, isn't it?'

'If you say so, Hugh.' The professor contrived a tired smile. 'Now, what about this offending object?' He indicated the infected eye.

If the 'blind' eye had taken a while to examine, the infected eye took much longer. With the special attachments to his ophthalmascope and other instruments Sir Hugh took several pictures of the eye and surrounding area, some of which he saved for his records.

He said, 'I'm going to treat this eye initially with Protargol ten per cent twice daily, as well as frequent bathing with saline or boracic solution. But after two days, Nurse, I want you to start applying this with an undine three times a day.' He held up a vial of liquid. 'It's pretty new stuff. It's had clinical trials and now we're trying it out in the department for this sort of condition—very successfully too. I think five days should see us through this particular difficulty, James, if your clever nurse can prevent a spread of infection.'

At last he had finished.

'At the moment, and largely due to your quick action and high standards of optical hygiene,' said Sir Hugh, addressing Emma, 'there's no keratitis. But it's a small miracle that it hasn't occurred, with such a severe attack of suppurating conjunctivitis—the cornea so quickly becomes involved. If it does, of course, there's the almost certain chance of a corneal ulcer forming.'

At last Emma was able to escort the consultant and his registrar through the dusky twilight to the bay and the waiting helicopter. It stood waiting, like a giant bird, ready to take to the skies.

There were a few more frustrating minutes spent in repeating goodbyes and confirming that everything would be done as instructed, before Emma could move away as the helicopter rose into the air. Only good manners and the knowledge that the two men had come a long way to attend to James kept her on the beach long enough to wave as the helicopter turned and skimmed away over the bay.

She was dying to get back to James. There was a lot to do before bedtime—the new treatment to start, and a sedative and pain-killing injection to give last thing at night. Thank goodness Sir Hugh had insisted upon something to help James sleep tonight. After this it would be at her discretion. She had to thank the ophthalmic surgeon for making it plain to her patient that he might need sedation occasionally over the next day or so, and that she or Dr MacLeod would be the judges of that need.

Doctors, she thought, like nurses, do not make good

patients. James would be the first to prescribe sedation and or pain-killers for someone in his condition.

It was nearly two hours later before she bathed and sank exhausted into her bed. Everything she could do for James had been done. She'd left a bell by his bed with instructions that he must ring it if he needed anything during the night.

He had made an attempt at joking when she had said that. 'Anything, dear girl?' he'd said, catching her hand after she'd given him his night injection. 'I might take you up on that.'

He'd looked incredibly handsome in maroon silk pyjamas and eye patches, with his crisp black hair with the white streak combed back into a thick wavy mass.

She'd retorted, with a laugh to cheer him, 'If you can manage to get out of bed in ten minutes' time I'm all yours!'

'What a cruel girl you are,' he responded with a smile. 'You know that——' he pointed in the direction of the empty syringe in her hand '—will knock me out in the next few minutes.'

Emma laughed again. 'You do surprise me,' she said.

He was asleep before she left the room. She went out, leaving the door ajar, and before sliding into her own bed she opened her door a few inches, knowing that she would hear him if he called or rang.

She fell asleep at last, just as the wind and rain which had been forecast started to buffet the windows. It seemed a fitting ending to an emotional and exhausting day. The change in the weather was appropriately matching events within the Old House.

# CHAPTER EIGHT

THE next few days were difficult. James, unused to either sedation or pain-killers, was half drowsy much of the time, but reluctant to give in to his condition. He had promised Sir Hugh that he wouldn't try to work for at least three days, and he honoured that promise. But inactivity, both of mind and body, he found irksome, to say the least, and Emma was hard put to it to fill the time for him satisfactorily.

Reading and discussing the post and giving him his first treatment of the day took a while, but generally she was finished by half-past ten. They made desultory conversation over coffee, discussed the news on the television and in the paper, and tackled the crossword puzzle.

Dr MacLeod called in twice a day and relieved the monotony for James by giving him a run-down of his visits and surgery work. In fact, the GP had no compunction in picking the professor's brains over a ticklish problem he was having with a couple of patients.

Emma worried that she seemed not to be able to keep the professor interested in anything. Gone was the wonderful rapport that had been building up between them prior to the infection. Now she realised that this had been largely due to work and their mutual interest in it, with only a limited time each day to indulge in other interests or conversation. The gap between his kind of life and the one that she had led was now obvious; they had, she thought sadly, little or nothing in common.

Ruthlessly she squashed the vague tentative hopes that she had harboured of a closer relationship developing between them. There was no future for them except as employer-patient and nurse-secretary, and the sooner she accustomed herself to that, the better.

It was no comfort that both Dr MacLeod and Mrs Mac praised her repeatedly for keeping the professor occupied and quiet, telling her that she had performed a miracle and no one else could have achieved so much. She just didn't believe them.

It was a joy, though, to treat his eyes. By the second day there was an improvement in the infected eye, the lids less puffy and a less virulent discharge apparent. The pain, too, was less marked, the professor assured her, and he refused pain-killers for the first time on the third morning. This was the day when Emma was to start the new treatment. It would take longer to deal with, as the 'magic' lotion was to be dispensed slowly via an undine. The fluid, Sir Hugh had stipulated, must be used both as an irrigant and an *in situ* healing agent.

'Undine—what's an undine?' Mrs Mac had asked when enquiring after the professor's treatment and welfare.

'It's a glass flask with a long spout. It makes it possible to control the amount of fluid being used,' Emma had explained.

'Oh, yes; I seem to remember the old doctor using one of those.'

Two days later Emma uncovered the infected eye. The professor said quietly, trying to steady his voice, 'Emma, I can see you plainly—no, slightly blurred, but much clearer. The best ever.' His voice trembled and rose a little from its usual low drawl. 'Emma—my God, you're beautiful! Your silver hair—I can see it properly now. My darling girl, it's worked! Hugh's bloody miracle stuff has worked! I'll have this patch off in no time.'

She had never seen him so elated, so full of a joy that he was valiantly trying to batten down. She had a job to contain herself, but knew that she must keep her emotions under control and persuade James to do the same. High emotion, however happy, could increase pressure. One of the factors in optical care was creating and maintaining calm.

She said with difficulty, in her most professional voice, hating to pour cold water over his high spirits, 'James, please calm down. You know it isn't good for you to get too excited. I'll just finish instilling the lotion and put a protective dressing over, before notifying Hector. He'll want to know what's happened and let Sir Hugh have the good news.'

He allowed her to complete the treatment with deceptive meekness. When she had finished he caught at her hands and pulled her to him. 'Emma. . .' his voice was husky '. . .you know how I feel about you. . .'

The phone rang and she tugged herself away from his imprisoning hold. She wasn't sure that she could have resisted him had he followed up his words and gesture with anything more intimate.

Astonishingly it was Sir Hugh on the phone, enquiring about his patient. Emma was able to give the good news, which he received with suitable pleasure, though without surprise. 'I thought something might break today,' he said cheerfully. 'Seems to be the pattern with this stuff.'

Emma handed the receiver over to James, who was full of praise for his friend's expertise, and gratitude with the result.

As soon as Sir Hugh had finished the call Emma got through to Hector's surgery before James could pursue his earlier conversation. She felt that they had both had enough emotional stress for the moment. He had come so close to saying what she longed to hear, but her lack of confidence where intimate relationships were concerned made her still veer away from him. He might, after all, only feel the way he did because of his euphoria over his eyes, and even a sophisticated patient like James was not above falling in love with his nurse. So she reasoned while they waited for Hector to arrive.

She fetched their coffee and, to divert him, said, 'By the way, you promised to tell me how your accident happened.'

'Did I really?' he asked in a teasing voice, fully aware of her intention to keep him off any intimacies.

'Yes.'

He laughed softly. 'You're very transparent, Emma, taking avoiding action. Do you really want to know?'

'Of course.'

'It was a hand grenade,' he said. 'I was being driven away from a leper colony in Sri Lanka when a guerrilla group, possibly Tamils, attacked the jeep. There was a lot of firing, then someone threw the grenade, and quite honestly I don't remember much of what happened after that.'

'You lost consciousness?'

'For several days, apparently. This,' he gestured towards his eyes, 'was the result. I was lucky. The driver, poor devil, was killed.'

'So who rescued you?'

'Ah, that's the sixty-four thousand dollar question. It might have been the guerrillas themselves. Anyway, somebody delivered me back to the colony—left me on the steps of the clinic. That's it really. The only other problem from my point of view was that I'd picked up this bug from somewhere *en route*, and it caused extra difficulties.'

Emma said, 'You make it sound very prosaic.'

'Well, it was in a way. I sometimes think that the British are the only people left who are surprised by violence of this sort, in spite of the news programmes telling us what's going on in the big wide world.'

Hector arrived at that moment and professed himself delighted with the condition of James's hitherto 'bad' eye. Emma told him that Sir Hugh had phoned and knew of the development, but would still like a word with Hector after he had examined the eye.

'I'll do that later, from home,' said Hector.

James admitted to being suddenly tired after Hector's departure, and amazingly opted to have a restful afternoon and evening.

'I expect you've plenty to be getting on with, Emma,' he said coolly, though she imagined that his eyes were possibly twinkling, for there was a smile in his voice. 'We'll be back into our full stride tomorrow, if that suits you.'

Another change of mood, thought Emma, or he's presenting another face. Perhaps he's punishing me for not falling into his arms immediately. She dismissed that idea almost as soon as it emerged. James, whatever his faults, was not small-minded. If he wanted to obliterate or reduce the effect of his emotional outburst when he'd rediscovered his sight he'd have found some way of saying so.

It quite suddenly occurred to her that his present reticence was on her account. With the extra-sensory perception that his blindness had bestowed on him, plus the Celtic fey quality that so many islanders seemed to possess, he might have divined her reservations. The idea that he was cool because of her feelings was reassuring.

'You're quite right, I've a lot to do,' she said cheerfully.

He was his distant self still the following morning. There was a lot of post to deal with, and he couldn't wait to start work after his recent inactivity—further evidence, Emma decided, that a working ethos was the cornerstone of their relationship. Her idea that James's reticence in pursuing his attentions towards her was on her account had evaporated.

She had just finished treating James's eyes when the phone rang. It was Angus, from Inverness.

'I've got a few days off,' he told Emma,' and so has Philippa. We'll be home the day after tomorrow, Saturday. Let Mrs Mac know, will you, so that she can get our rooms ready and so on and provide one of her stupendous meals? We're both half starved!'

He put the phone down before she could tell him of James's recent set-back and rapid recovery.

The professor had recognised his brother's voice.

'Well, what does my mad young brother want now,' he asked, 'apart from your company?'

Ridiculously his comment made Emma blush.

'It's nothing like that,' she protested. 'Both he and Philippa have got time off and are coming to Skye.'

'Well, that's the end of our quiet existence for a bit, Emma,' said the professor, and she couldn't tell if he was pleased at the prospect or not.

Something of a bombshell was to fall before the day was out. It was early afternoon when the phone rang again and a female voice asked for James.

'Who shall I say is calling?' asked Emma.

'Nesta.'

James must have heard the reply, for he all but snatched the receiver from Emma's hand.

'James here,' he said briefly, harshly.

Emma moved off the terrace and wandered round the garden. She had no doubt that this caller was also the writer of the letter several days earlier.

She stayed away for about a quarter of an hour. Somehow the voice of the caller and James's response to it seemed to indicate that a long and angry conversation might ensue.

When she returned James had left the terrace, but she could hear his voice, not loud but staccato with controlled rage, coming from the study. At first she thought he was still on the telephone, but he wasn't. He heard her coming, and he broke off his conversation to call her into the room.

To her surprise, Emma found that it was Mrs Mac who was on the receiving end of the professor's diatribe. She was standing in front of him, lips pursed tightly together, hands concealed in her rolled-up kitchen apron.

The housekeeper turned a relieved face towards Emma. 'Now, hold your whist, Master Jamie,' she said to the professor, cutting ruthlessly across his words. 'Miss Emma here will deal with the problem in its entirety, will ye not?' she asked, but it was a rhetorical question. Clearly she had no doubt that Emma would know how to deal with their irate employer.

'Well,' replied Emma, 'it would help if I knew what

the problem was.' She hoped that she sounded firm and reassuring, for both the professor and Mrs Mac needed calming down.

There was a moment's silence while James digested his housekeeper's remark, and then he capitulated graciously. He quelled his anger and turned a sardonic smile on them both. 'What am I, a poor helpless man, to do in the face of two strong-minded women but give in and seek their combined advice?'

Emma, pleased that he had calmed down a little and that Mrs Mac looked less uptight, said, deliberately sounding rather lost, 'I still don't know what it's all about.'

Rather wearily James said, 'It's about Nesta—the phone call, the letter the other day, remember?'

'Yes, I remember.'

'I thought I'd put her off, but I was wrong. She arrives with the children tomorrow evening.' He sounded panicky for a moment. 'Emma. . .' he turned an anxious face towards her '. . . I don't think I can stand a house full of people, especially Nesta and her brood.'

Her heart went out to him. Not only had he so recently recovered from a full-blown virus infection and near-blindness, but he had been fighting this sinister fatigue syndrome, and weathered the shock of a violent attack upon his person. Was it any wonder that he was reluctant to accept the responsibility of even his own children, with whom he had only limited contact? It seemed a reasonable excuse to explain his shying away from his responsibilities. After all, he was special, both to her and to hundreds of patients who had, or who might, rely upon him.

'Leave it to me,' she heard herself say firmly. 'I'll sort this out.'

She marched from the room, followed by Mrs Mac.

'I don't know what your intentions are, Miss Emma,' said the housekeeper, 'but I think that ye'll no catch up with that Nesta or the puir wee bairns before they arrive. No one knows where they're at the while.'

'Surely they're in France or Belgium, or wherever it is that they live? If I can phone them I can stop them before they start their journey.'

Mrs Mac looked on her pityingly. 'Nay, ye canna. They are somewhere *en route*, but not even the master knows where. She's too clever by half, that Nesta; didna let him know where she was heading for. I doubt ye can do a thing before they arrive.'

It was true. Emma asked for and received the phone number of the apartment on the Rue du Jardin des Olives, and rang the number several times over the rest of the day. There was no answer.

Late in the evening, after she had given James his treatment and they had had supper, she spoke to him about it.

'I'm sorry that I haven't been able to stop them coming,' she said sadly, feeling she had let him down badly, 'but I can't get hold of anyone at that address. Mrs Mac thinks that they're on the way.'

'Mrs Mac's right,' said James in a subdued voice. 'I'm afraid even you, dear girl, can't prevent this particular happening.' He braced himself. 'Anyway, once they're here the children will be OK, especially after Nesta goes away. They play up rather when she's around, but they soon settle down. You'll find them rather spoilt, but basically nice kids.' He stretched out

a hand and touched her arm. 'You won't let them drive
you away, Emma, will you?'

Emma was quite indignant.

'Of course not! What on earth do you take me for?
I'm your nurse and your secretary; I'm not going to
abandon my job because of a couple of spoilt children.
And perhaps their parents are more to blame than they
are. If they're shunted from pillar to post at the whim
of indifferent adults they may feel that they need to
rebel.'

To her surprise he agreed. He didn't seem to think
that she was including him in her condemnation of the
adults concerned. Surely, she thought when getting
ready for bed, he wasn't such a male chauvinist that he
considered it only the woman's job to care for the
children? She knew that he wouldn't be mean where
money or material matters were concerned, but, from
his attitude towards having the children stay, it seemed
that he was indifferent to his other responsibilities.

Emma was glad that Philippa and Angus were
coming. Surely they would help keep their niece and
nephew in order, even if they couldn't exercise any
control over their sister-in-law? It would be good for
James to have their company to relieve the boredom of
his situation.

It had been nice of him to pretend that he was happy
with just the two of them together, but she was sure
that he must find her limited social attributes boring.
She couldn't say funny or clever things to order. With
people like the MacLeods, with whom she had a
professional rapport, she knew that she could hold her
own, but when a Colonel and Mrs Pierce had come for
drinks one evening she had been a complete disaster.

She'd hardly dared to open her mouth. Their entire

conversation had been about places like Singapore and Hong Kong, and the delights of living abroad with servants on tap all the time. In fact she'd had the distinct feeling that they had considered that she should have been below stairs, or wherever employees belonged.

True, the professor had included her in the conversation whenever possible, but she thought that it had probably been a strain for him, and the evening had highlighted the difference between her background and his. When they had stood on the porch, waving good-bye to the departing guests, he had muttered something in Gaelic. When Emma had asked him what it was he had apologised, laughed and said it was better that she did not know.

He had flung an arm round her shoulder and suggested that they went for their delayed walk along the shore. She had known, though, that, in spite of his gesture and seeming pleasure in her company, he had longed for more stimulating and intellectual pleasures.

Well, he would soon have his brother and sister, and Nesta and family, to provide that. However angry he had been when Nesta had phoned, she must at one time have represented all that he desired in a woman. Perhaps he was reluctant to have her in the house because he hated to be reminded of what he had lost?

Emma viewed their arrival with foreboding, but was determined to support the professor, whatever happened. In a flight of fancy, steeling herself to accept the fact that there could never be anything between herself and James, she even cast herself in the role of peacemaker between him and Nesta. After all, his happiness was all that mattered.

Surely yesterday, when he had touched her so tend-

erly and seemed about to speak with intimacy, was
only a temporary lapse on his part? She couldn't, and
wouldn't, believe that it was a true indication of his
feelings for her. Too much suggested otherwise. He
was just a frustrated, clever man, condemned at present to a restricted lifestyle and dependent on her for
companionship.

She went to bed after an exhausting and emotional
day and, unexpectedly, slept well.

The next morning started badly. They were all in a
state of uncomfortable anticipation over the arrival
later in the day of Nesta and the children. Mrs Mac,
whom Emma had seldom seen ruffled, was terribly
agitated.

'The bairns have always had the auld night nursery,'
she said, waylaying Emma at the head of the stairs as
she was about to go down for breakfast. 'But they're
thirteen now and should, do ye not think, have each
their own room?'

It surprised Emma to learn that they were just in
their teens. For some reason she had thought them to
be seven or eight.

Although she didn't want the professor put under
any extra strain, she thought that he would have to
adjudicate on this one.

He frowned when asked what to do about the rooms.

'Well, I suppose they each need a room of their own
now,' he said irritably. 'For God's sake, Mrs Mac,
there are plenty to choose from in this pile. Put them
where you like—their mother can hardly complain, if
she will insist on dumping them here year after year.'

Mrs Mac saw the horrified look on Emma's face.
'He's very fond of them,' she said hastily, taking

Emma's arm and almost dragging her from the study, 'but it's a very trying time for him.'

'You're telling me!' replied Emma angrily, for the first time feeling out of tune with the housekeeper's devotion to her master. 'After all, there are limits even for someone as important and useful to society as the professor. Even he must accept some responsibility for——'

The rest of her words were cut off by a shrill scream from the kitchen. Both she and Mrs Mac rushed to see what had happened.

They were met in the doorway by Oona, crying noisily and waving around a hand dripping blood all over the floor.

Emma caught Oona's arm and held it aloft. There was a cut across the palm of the girl's hand.

'Get me a clean towel, Mrs Mac,' said Emma, still holding Oona's arm high. She pushed the kitchen-maid down on to a chair. 'Tell me what happened.'

'It was the big knife of Mistress Mac's—the sharp one for fish and things. I thought to cut some bread and it slipped.' She turned agonised eyes to Emma. 'Will I be losing my hand, miss?'

'What, from a little scratch like that?' she said, deliberately scathing to reassure the girl. 'No, I'll just bandage it up with a pad over the cut to stop the bleeding. Mrs Mac, will you hold this arm up, please, while I fetch some things from the surgery?'

Emma was relieved to find the study empty. Either the professor had gone upstairs again or he was already at breakfast in the dining-room.

She collected an antiseptic and pain-killing spray, a sachet of pre-packed dressings and micropore tape, and a plastic glove.

It took only a few minutes to apply the spray and dressing and cover with the plastic glove. Blood was already congealing on the long but shallow cut. Knowing that James had ensured that all his staff were regularly given anti-tetanus jabs and top-ups, Emma had no worries about the long-term consequences. She suggested to Mrs Mac that Oona should do light work for the morning to avoid splitting open the wound.

Mrs Mac was not too pleased. There was a lot of extra work to be done with the arrival of Nesta and the children that evening, and Philippa and Angus the following day.

'Don't worry, Mrs Mac, I'll give a hand with beds and getting the rooms ready. The professor has a lot of tape-listening to do before I can catch up on my typing. Once I've seen to his eyes I shall be all yours.'

Need and reluctance to let someone she considered a guest of the master help with domestic work warred for supremacy in Mrs Mac's face for a brief moment. Then, being a practical woman, she agreed to accept Emma's help.

'But I dinna know what Master Jamie will say. He'll no like ye doing these chores.'

Emma wanted to say that he would have to lump it, but instead made reassuring noises and pointed out to the housekeeper that nurses spent half their lives making beds of one sort or another.

'And,' she added, 'I'll tell him that I'm doing the flowers and collecting the vegetables from Auld Mac if he gets too inquisitive. After all, there's really no need for him to know exactly what I'm doing.'

Mrs Mac was reasonably satisfied with this arrangement, and Emma went off to the dining-room and a belated breakfast. The professor was just about to leave.

'You're late,' he said tersely as Emma entered.

Emma struck while the iron was hot. 'A little problem in the kitchen,' she explained. 'Oona cut herself on a kitchen knife. Nothing serious, but she'll be a bit restricted for an hour or so. I thought I might give Mrs Mac a hand with the flowers and things, to help out. She's a bit stretched with the visitors arriving and so on. It'll give you time to listen to the tapes and add anything you feel necessary before I type them up. Of course, I'll see to your treatment first.'

The professor growled. 'For that, I suppose, I should be grateful.'

Emma clenched her teeth and refused to rise to the bait. *If,* she thought, *you'd made better arrangements for your family we wouldn't be in this mess.*

James asked suddenly in a quiet, concerned voice, 'Is Oona all right? She's rather a walking disaster, I'm afraid. Gets it from her mother. She was a clumsy soul, though full of goodwill.'

Emma was as always surprised at the depth of knowledge and interest that James displayed in connection with his employees. He seemed to be aware of all their little foibles from generations back. She supposed that it was the Scottish equivalent of *noblesse oblige.*

His eyes were continuing to respond to treatment. Both were infinitely improved from a few days earlier. She knew that Sir Hugh would be delighted at their progress, and said so to James.

He was thrilled with his improving sight in the eye that had caused so much concern when the optic nerve had been at risk. It made up in some measure for the trying situation that was developing over the imminent arrival of Nesta and the children.

Emma settled him in the study with tapes and tape-recorder and went off to help Mrs Mac. What a pity, she thought as she made her way upstairs, that James didn't exhibit the same concern for his family as he did for his staff. He showed such warmth and compassion where they were concerned.

She recalled his gentle manner with Auld Mac when he had pronged his foot. She wondered how a man of such tenderness with patients, repeatedly revealed on tapes and videos, could be so indifferent where those closest to him were involved. And why, she mused, was someone like Mrs Mac almost hostile to his estranged wife, though compassionate towards young Jamie and Bess, 'the puir wee bairns'?

She was reluctant to sound Mrs Mac out too deeply about the expected visitors—it rather smacked of prying behind James's back. But, now that their arrival was imminent, surely she would be given some information about them, if only because their presence would have some effect on her patient and his routine?

But nothing was forthcoming from James, and in the end, even if she was going to bring herself to discuss matters with Mrs Mac, Emma was denied the opportunity. The phone went a couple of times and she answered it and took messages. Later a tradesman called, and Emma suggested to Mrs Mac that she stayed down in the kitchen, where there was much to do, while she carried on preparing the rooms.

It had been decided that Jamie and Bess were to have the schoolroom and the little room opening off it, where at one time the nanny used to sleep. She prettied up the small room for Bess with a posy of flowers from the garden. There seemed no reason why the girl should not benefit from such a simple little extra. After all, it wasn't her fault that her parents were separated and apparently at loggerheads.

After seeing to the children's rooms and a large double room in the same corridor for their mother, Emma carried on with her bed-making in Philippa's and Angus's rooms. At least poor hard-pressed Mrs Mac wouldn't have to worry about the upstairs work, and, by the afternoon, Oona would be able to help her properly in the kitchen.

It was lunchtime before she had finished, and cold meat and salad with jacket potatoes awaited her and the professor in the dining-room. The weather had well and truly broken; wind and flurries of rain battered the terrace where only days before they had baked in the sunshine.

James was in a good mood. His morning's work was, as he put it, 'fruitful'.

'There's plenty for you to type up, Emma,' he told her cheerfully as they sat down at the table. He seemed to have shed the worries of the morning, and Emma envied him the ability to set his problems aside and concentrate on the work that he loved.

Their conversation was of a general nature during lunch, or concerned with the tapes she was to work on. No mention was made of the forthcoming visitors. It was as if they didn't exist.

After lunch Emma performed the small chores necessary to make the professor comfortable, and took herself off to her office.

It was nearly four o'clock when Oona announced that she had taken the tea-tray into the study. Emma joined the professor there, amazed that the time had passed so quickly and that she too had managed to block out the unpleasant problems and concentrate on work.

She found herself actually enjoying her tea and Mrs Mac's delicious gingerbread, hot and spread with butter, the first food that she hadn't had to force down since learning of Nesta's visit.

There was still time to do some more typing before the visitors arrived or the evening routine began.

'I'm going back to my office, James,' she told him. 'I can finish that tape in a short while.'

'Must you?' he asked. 'I thought we might have a wee while together before the Teutonic hordes descend upon us.'

'Teutonic?' queried Emma.

'Nesta is half-German-Swiss, a quarter French, a quarter English. The children were born in Switzerland.'

'Oh, I see,' she replied. But she didn't see really—either why he was telling her this, or why it mattered.

He was about to speak again, but she interrupted him. 'There's no need, Professor,' she said, sounding and feeling very formal, for without being formal she couldn't have kept her emotions at bay. 'It really has nothing to do with me. I've said that I'll stay and look after you; complete my two months' contract at least, both as nurse and secretary. I don't break my promises.'

She left the room on wobbly legs and was glad that he couldn't see them.

'Emma,' she heard him call as she shut herself into her office. She didn't look back, or answer. Enough is enough, she thought. Isn't it sufficient to be in love with one's employer, without having to discuss his wife—separated, ex or still legitimately his—with him?

She steeled herself not to think about what he might have said to her had she stayed to listen. She had deliberately avoided moments of intimacy over the last few days, always conscious of her confused thoughts about James. For the most part, he too had been rather withdrawn, though not in the least unfriendly; in fact, he seemed almost to be enjoying some secret knowledge that even the imminent arrival of Nesta and the children couldn't spoil.

Well, she knew what her reasons were for avoiding close contact, but would not let herself wonder too deeply about his. It's like endlessly counting cherry stones on a plate, she thought—he loves me, he loves me not.

She was still in her office typing furiously when there was a tap at the door and Mrs Mac entered.

'The visitors have arrived,' she announced. 'Will you come along and greet them?' Her tone was gentle, compassionate.

She knows, thought Emma, that I'm in love with the professor. She squared her shoulders and turned to face the housekeeper.

'Of course I'll come, Mrs Mac. Lead the way.'

# CHAPTER NINE

BOTH Nesta and the children were a surprise to Emma. She hadn't formed any particular picture of them in her mind, but had somehow thought that Nesta would be blonde and rather Nordic in appearance, and the children dark like their father. In fact, all three were brilliant auburn-haired beauties. Even young Jamie, who would undoubtedly abhor the suggestion of beauty, was staggeringly handsome.

Nesta was tall and willowy with a wealth of red-gold hair streaming down her back in a rippling cascade. Bess's abundant hair was restrained into a luxuriant plait, swinging heavily like a ship's rope to her waist. Jamie's hair, brushed back vigorously from a high forehead, was thick and wavy in a mane that reached almost to the neck of his T-shirt.

'Ah, Emma, there you are,' said the professor in a well-modulated voice, almost entirely devoid of expression. 'Come in and meet Mrs Nesta Leroux and her children.'

For one extraordinary moment Emma thought she was going to faint, something she had never done in her life before. With a tremendous effort she regained control of her shaking limbs and stepped forward to shake Mrs Leroux by the hand. The relief at learning that whatever relationship the lady had had with James in the past didn't include marriage in the present was astonishing. If Mrs Nesta Leroux had had any claims on the professor she clearly had renounced them in favour of another marriage.

Emma wanted to cheer. Instead she smiled pleasantly at the auburn-haired woman. 'Did you have a good journey?' she asked.

'Well, it was only from Liège,' replied Nesta, looking surprised. 'Hardly significant.'

At any other time Emma would have blushed with discomfort at this dismissive answer to a civil question, but she was still elated by the knowledge that Mrs Leroux was not Mrs MacDonald.

James said, 'Let me introduce Bess and Jamie.'

Emma held out her hand to each of them in turn and received limp, indifferent handshakes from them both, and an unintelligible mumble in return for her own warm welcome. It was a great pity to find such lovely-looking children so sullen.

Mrs Mac asked if she would take the 'wee bairns' upstairs to tidy up before supper.

'Oh, surely,' said Nesta, 'you have enough to do in the kitchen? Nurse here can see to the children.'

There was a gasp from Mrs Mac, who gave the professor a horrified glance. Emma looked at him too and was shocked at the anger in his face. When he spoke it was in such a cold, steely voice that she almost shivered.

'Off with you, kids, with Mrs Mac, and don't come down till you're called.'

It was a good job, thought Emma, that James couldn't see their mutinous faces, or the malicious, tight little smile on their mother's face. Nesta had meant to be offensive. It wasn't her words but the arrogant way in which she had uttered them that made them so unpleasant. Whether or not she was aware of

Emma's true position in the house there was no way of knowing. She had wanted to sound insulting, but whether to diminish Emma herself or annoy James wasn't clear.

She had intimated in her letter that James couldn't be as ill as she'd been led to believe. Perhaps she genuinely thought that Emma was here in an au pair capacity rather than as a trained nursing sister?

No, her manner was more deliberately rude than could be ascribed to a mistake like that. She would know that any nanny worth her salt would have walked out if provoked in that way.

Mrs Mac hustled the grumbling children out before her. The silence in the room became even more leaden. Even Nesta began to look a little uneasy as she and Emma both stared at James. He stood, straight as a ramrod, in front of the log fire that had been lit against the chill of the stormy evening. The white streak in his hair was very marked, his lean face lined, his lips compressed tightly. He waited until the door closed behind the exiting party.

'Now,' he barked in a ferocious voice, turning his head in Nesta's direction, and making both her and Emma jump, 'you will apologise to Emma, at once!'

Nesta was flustered. She had gone quite pale. Emma tried to say that she didn't mind being mistaken for a nanny, but it came out in a muddled, incoherent mess, and James ignored it anyway.

'Well?' he rasped, rapping the parquet floor with his stick. 'I'm waiting.'

'But, James——'

'No buts, Nesta. If you don't apologise within the next thirty seconds I'll have you and the children shipped down to the hotel tonight, and off the island tomorrow.'

For one moment Emma thought that Nesta was going to call his bluff, if indeed it was bluff, but suddenly she turned towards Emma and spoke in a low voice. 'Sorry about that, Nurse——'

'Miss Seymour,' interrupted the professor.

'Miss Seymour. I'm afraid I mistook you for someone engaged by the professor to look after the children.'

'Not good enough,' said James in clippped tones. 'That's only half an apology; let's hear a proper one.'

'Oh, please, James,' said Emma. 'It's enough.'

'Not for me it isn't. Nesta?'

'I apologise unreservedly,' said Nesta in a resigned fashion.

'That's better.' The professor sat down heavily in his chair. 'Now, if you'd like to go up to your room and unpack or whatever, Emma can see to my treatment before supper. Mrs Mac will let you and the children know when it's ready.' He sounded infinitely weary.

Emma was surprised at his dismissal of Nesta, and even more surprised at her acceptance of his authority. She made no attempt to argue or plead with him, just left the room with drooping shoulders and an air of defeat.

When she had gone James said softly, 'Emma, I'm so sorry about that—I had no idea that Nesta was going to be so vindictive. Please forgive me for putting you in that position.'

'Oh, please, just let's forget it. I wish you hadn't made such an issue over it. I don't know how we're going to face each other again.'

'My dear girl, don't worry on that score. Whatever

act Nesta's putting on at this moment she'll have shed by suppertime. She's got a skin like a rhinoceros.'

'But I haven't. It was just too embarrassing for words, the way you put her down in front of me. It was cruel!'

'Well, I'm damned! Would you rather, dear heart,' he said with heavy sarcasm, 'that I'd let her get away with it?'

'I don't know, I just don't know. I don't think I understand about people like you, and the sort of life you lead.'

'Emma, my darling girl, come here.' He sounded arrogant, imperative. 'No, I mean, please come here. Let me try to explain about Nesta.'

He held out both his hands in a supplicating gesture.

Slowly she walked towards him. What, she wondered, could he say that would explain that lady's position in his scheme of things? Why was she able to come and go more or less as she liked, and yet be subject to his authority? For the way that she had succumbed to his will when he had ordered her to apologise was extraordinary. Even the children's reactions had been strange. It was obvious that they were wilful and used to having their own way, yet they had accepted James's order that they should leave the room with only muted rebellion.

'Oh, Emma!' James said as she reached him. To her astonishment, and before she could resist, he pulled her down on to his lap. 'My dearest girl.' He put a hand up to her head and pressed it down until their lips met. 'I love you so much,' he whispered. 'So very much.'

His lips were hard and hurtful on hers. She returned his passionate kisses with all the emotion that she had been storing up over the past weeks. For a wild moment disbelief swamped her. Had she heard correctly, and, if she had, did he mean it? She realised that she didn't care; it was enough to be in his arms, even if he was using her to assuage his feelings for the beautiful Nesta.

Over and over again, his words muffled as he pressed his lips to hers, he repeated, 'I love you, I love you.'

Emma mumbled back, 'I love you too, darling, so much.'

His hands slipped beneath her loose cotton sweater and caressed her bare breasts, until her nipples were erect with longing.

'The surgery,' he murmured. 'Safe there. Come, my love.' He stood up and put an arm round her waist, and, for all his blindness, it was he who guided her to the door of the surgery.

As they reached the door the phone started ringing.

'Leave it,' he said thickly.

Emma couldn't. Her professional training could not let her ignore what might be as much a call for help as a social call.

She barely had time to say that she was speaking from Professor MacDonald's residence before the caller, with a foreign accent, said in her ear, 'It is imperative that I speak to the professor immediately. I speak from Sri Lanka.'

Emma put the receiver into the professor's hand. 'You must answer it, James,' she said. 'It's someone speaking from Sri Lanka. It sounds urgent.'

James took the receiver from her and said calmly, 'MacDonald here. Can I help?'

The call took some time. Emma realised from the replies James was giving that it related to the last case he had dealt with before his accident. She found the appropriate file and stood ready to read it to him should he need information. In the event, with just a minor reminder, his fantastic memory served him well, and he was able to give the necessary help to the caller.

The telephone call quite naturally shattered the intimacy that had built up between them. When James finally put down the receiver all passion had fled and they both knew it. It was he who said, 'Another time, darling, God and our patients willing.'

He touched her arm and trailed his hand down to her wrist. Turning her hand over, he raised it to his lips and kissed it tenderly.

Emma found herself at a loss for words and sought comfort in professionalism. She gave him his treatment, cleared up the surgery, and went off to shower and change for the evening. With difficulty she got herself under control and went down to the dining-room, mentally preparing herself for anything that might occur.

To her surprise, the evening passed off rather well. Mrs Mac had risen to the occasion and presented them with a superb meal. Even the visitors, who she expected were used to good food, couldn't fault the fare on the table that evening. Freshly dug potatoes from the garden, buttered and minted, accompanied by lamb casserole, asparagus, new peas and baby carrots. Nothing exotic, but perfectly cooked and served on plain white, thin porcelain plates banded with silver. The main course was followed by raspberry tart and cream, coffee, liqueurs, biscuits and cheese and fresh fruit.

The children remained quiet and morose, though they both tucked into the food with obvious enjoyment.

Nesta was politeness itself to Emma, including her in the conversation, which was mostly about a recent trip to Paris.

James was a perfect host, sending the children away to watch television when they had finished eating, before they had a chance to get bored. When both Emma and Nesta refused any more to eat or drink he suggested that they moved to the sitting-room.

Once there, he sat down at the piano and started to play—first a bit of jazz, and then some excerpts from musicals, ending with a few Noël Coward favourites, in which he imitated 'the Master' with great skill.

Emma, trying not to let her love show too plainly in front of Nesta, feasted her eyes upon James as he sat at the piano. After a few minutes he suggested casually, 'Emma, come and play a duet with me.' He moved along the stool to make room for her. To her fury, she couldn't stop herself shivering as she sat down beside him, revelling in his closeness.

He was wearing spectacles with one opaque and one transparent lens, and his unshielded violet eye gleamed mischievously. 'Chilly, my dear?' he asked.

Noting a strange look on Nesta's face, Emma made a tremendous effort to pull herself together. 'A little,' she said as carelessly as possible. 'After all, the weather has changed dramatically, hasn't it?'

'Oh, dramatically,' James replied with a wolfish grin.

Emma, realising that Nesta was determined to get James to herself, excused herself just after this incident, and retired to her room.

She got ready for bed in a dream-like state, her mind entirely filled with James and the wonderful, ecstatic, mind-blowing thing that had happened between them. She had thought herself in love before, once seriously, but nothing had produced this euphoria. No one had ever made her tremble by simply being close, as he had tonight. No one except James had ever been able to read her mind, sense her reactions, as he did.

'I could have danced all night,' she hummed to herself, twirling round the room before falling with a laugh on to her bed. Immediately she wondered what it would be like to dance with James. She had heard that he was an excellent Highland dancer; was he also any good at disco or old-fashioned ballroom dancing? How would it feel to be held close to his wide chest and be waltzed or tangoed round the dance-floor?

Her imagination went into overdrive as she thought of those long, slender fingers teasing her into awareness as they had that afternoon in the study. He had said 'I love you' several times, and had seemed to mean it. Her high excitement began to fade a little. Perhaps the frustrations and celibate existence that he had been forced to lead recently, and the reminder in the letter of his old love, the beautiful Nesta, had triggered off his actions.

No, he had professed an interest in her before Nesta had communicated. And he had kissed her with such restrained passion tonight when he had escorted her to the foot of the stairs. She sighed and at last fell asleep.

Emma's sleep was full of disturbing dreams, and, only an hour or so after she had retired to bed, she woke suddenly. She found that her mind was full of Nesta and her association with James. She realised that she had built up a whole history concerning Nesta, the professor and the children.

Now she realised that much, if not all of it, might be just the result of her imaginings. Certainly the professor had a vast influence over Nesta and her family; and certainly Mrs Mac and James's brother and sister resented the Leroux ménage, but they had not said why. Emma herself had provided answers—wrong answers, possibly. If the phone had not rung as she and James had entered the treatment-room this afternoon she might by now be fully in the picture. Or maybe not, she thought, grinning wryly at the picture of what might have taken place between them if a crisis in Sri Lanka had not intervened.

She giggled a bit hysterically. Where, she wondered, in the sterile surroundings of the treatment-room would they have made love? On the narrow surgical chair? On the pristine, polished, clinically clean floor? James had said it would be 'safe' there, she recalled. He had meant from intruders, but Emma, reviewing what might have been in the comfort of her bedroom after a trying day, wondered just what he might have meant by 'safe'!

Her wayward thoughts were interrupted by a scratching at the door. Cautiously she moved towards it. Could it possibly be James? she wondered.

'Who is it?'

'Bess. I feel so ill.'

Emma flung open the door. The child, whey-faced and shivering, stood in the corridor.

Emma pulled her gently into the room.

'I'm going to be sick,' said Bess, and vomited all over the carpet. 'I'm sorry, I'm sorry,' she wailed.

'Don't be, love; better up than in,' Emma reassured her. 'Now, come through to the bathroom and wash your face, and take off those soiled pyjamas. I'll lend you something.'

Bess, already looking a little better after being sick, allowed herself to be directed to the bathroom. By the time Emma had returned and knocked on the door, offering a short nightdress and panties, Bess had almost recovered her usual truculence. She snatched the nightclothes from Emma's hands.

'I can go back to my room now,' she said stiffly. 'Sorry I bothered you.'

'It's no bother, Bess,' countered Emma softly. 'I am a nurse, you know, and used to this sort of thing.' She gestured to the evil-smelling mess on the floor. 'It won't take a minute to clear up.' She smiled, hoping to reassure the girl, who, though improved, still looked off-colour. 'Look, Bess, I think you'd better pop into my bed for a while. You may want to throw up again— you look as if you might.'

For a moment she thought that Bess was going to refuse, but all of a sudden the small, pretty face crumpled and she burst into tears. 'Yes, please,' she said tearfully. 'P'raps I'd better have a bowl.'

'Perhaps you had, Bess. What a sensible idea.'

It was while Emma was clearing up the mess that another timid knock came at the door. This time it was Jamie who stood in the corridor.

'Is Bess here?' he asked in his raspy, half-man, half-boy voice.

'Yes; come in.' Emma pulled the door wide open.

'Yuk!' he said with a snort, stepping over the mess. 'Did she do that?'

'Yes.'

The boy made a face. 'She kept being sick last week,' he said. 'She had a pain in her belly.' He obviously said 'belly' to try to shock her and let her know that he wasn't in the least perturbed by his sister's tendency to vomit; but his anxious face belied the bravado of his words.

Emma followed him to the bedside, where Bess lay holding the plastic bowl that Emma had found for her. She looked pale and drawn. Her magnificent abundance of hair, now unshackled from its plait, tumbled in wet tendrils round her face. As they reached her she suddenly groaned and drew her right leg up almost to her waist, at the same time clutching her abdomen.

'Did you say Bess has had a similar attack to this recently?' Emma asked Jamie.

He nodded. 'Several over the last couple of months. Our doctor thinks she might have what he called a grumbling appendix. He told Mummy that Bess ought to go into hospital for observation.'

Emma, who until that moment had believed Bess's vomiting due to a big meal on a traveller's stomach, was shocked. It was much more serious than that. Possibly the appendix was ruptured or about to rupture. They could be in for a full-blown abdominal emergency.

'Go and wake. . .' she hesitated for a moment '. . .the professor. Tell him I need him here.'

Jamie stood rooted to the spot, looking belligerent. 'I want——'

He got no further, for Emma pushed him towards the door. 'Unless you want to see your sister very ill indeed, or worse,' she said furiously, 'go and do as you're told. Then fetch your mother. Now, go!'

Jamie went, suddenly looking pale and defensive and very young. Emma heard him hammering on James's door before bursting in.

Within a minute or so James was at her side. He had removed his night shield and put on his dark glasses, but hadn't stopped to put on a dressing-gown over his Paisley silk pyjamas. It was amazing how wide awake and alert he was. Emma forgot that she too could flash from deep sleep to clear-witted awareness in seconds. It was all part of being a doctor or nurse.

She gave him the briefest history of Bess's condition. The girl was half comatose by now and groaning with pain. She had a temperature, though without going down to the surgery for a thermometer Emma could only guess that it was quite high. Her pulse-rate and respirations were rapid. Everything, in fact, tallied with a febrile condition associated with pain and possible infection.

'I'll examine her, please,' said James in a consultant-like voice.

'Certainly, Professor,' replied Emma, equally professional, turning back the bedclothes and pulling up the short nightdress to expose Bess's flat and rigid abdomen.

Being professional was, in fact, the only way they could contend with the situation, they were both so incensed by the few facts that had been given them about the child's condition. How could any mother have placed her child in jeopardy for the sake of pursuing her own plans? Emma wondered as she assisted James. Nesta had obviously done just this by making the journey to Skye.

Young Jamie arrived back in the room, panting from his run up and down the stairs to rouse his mother.

'I can't wake her up,' he said. 'She's taken her pills— she'll be dead to the world till the morning.' He sounded resigned.

'Go and ask Mrs Mac—gently, mind you—to kindly come down, Jamie,' asked James quietly, lifting his head to give the boy a smile.

'I have; I've done that, and she's coming any minute.'

The housekeeper arrived at that moment, bundled into a check dressing-gown, with her iron-grey hair dragged back in a sort of elderly pony-tail. But in spite of that she looked strong, reassuring and, above all, motherly. They all breathed a sigh of relief at her arrival.

James said in a cool, unemotional voice, 'Sorry to get you up, Mackie.' It was the first time that Emma had heard him use this nickname. 'Will you phone the Cottage Hospital? Tell them it's an emergency, a very ripe appendix. Say you're speaking for me and it's my god-daughter who's the patient. We'll have her there in. . .'

He glanced at Emma, who said with equal cool, 'Forty-five minutes.'

'. . .forty-five minutes, unless by some miracle there's an ambulance in the area. And when you've finished passing on all that, Mrs Mac, please ask the casualty officer if he'll have a word with me. Many thanks.'

He smiled again and the housekeeper returned his smile. They're a team too, thought Emma. They've come through many a crisis together.

'Right, Professor,' said Mrs Mac, not to be outdone in coolness. 'At once. And perhaps Master Jamie here,' she prodded young James gently, 'will give an auld lady a hand with making a cup of tea.'

'I'm going with Bess,' said Jamie. 'You can't stop me.'

'Who would want to, dear boy?' said the professor. 'Of course you'll come with us to the hospital.'

Pacified, Jamie left with Mrs Mac, and James, casting

Emma a conspiratorial look, continued his examination
of Bess.

He took off his dark glasses and peered at Bess to
test her reaction as he palpated her abdomen gently,
paying great attention to Munro's, or the more com-
monly called McBurney's point. As his long fingers
gently pressed the area between the spine of the iliac
and the navel Bess screwed up her face, obviously
reacting to the increased pain or discomfort.

'Not much doubt, Emma,' he said softly. 'The sooner
we can get her to Theatre and surgery the better.
Thank goodness nowadays we don't have to wait for
the stomach contents to clear. The anaesthetists have
got this neat gadget for preventing vomit being inhaled
into the lungs. Great invention—saves time and
distress.'

In spite of the gravity of the situation, Emma was in
a state of euphoria. It seemed almost indecent, in view
of Bess's condition, that she should feel elated, but she
couldn't help herself. His *god-daughter*; not his daughter, but his god-daughter. No wonder James felt great
concern for this family; however, it was not the ultimate responsibility of a parent. Emma now understood
James's ambivalent attitude to Nesta's untimely arrival.

Mrs Mac returned, carrying the mobile phone which
she proffered to James.

'I've explained everything,' she said. 'This is Dr
Frazer on the phone. She's the casualty officer on
duty.'

James nodded and took the implement from her.

'Dr Frazer,' he said in what Emma thought of as his
most conciliatory tone. 'My housekeeper has explained
the situation. I would like to ask your permission to

give this child a shot of pethidine. It will help her sustain the journey to the hospital. Is that in order?'

A muffled voice, obviously agreeing with the professor, could be heard. Emma gave him a sardonic smile as he put the phone down.

'Did you really think she might have had the guts to disagree with you?'

He grinned. 'I don't make a habit of pulling rank,' he said softly, 'but there are legitimate occasions, don't you think?'

'Certainly, and this is one of them.' She deliberately became brisk. 'Shall I go and get dressed while you're still here?'

'Yes, do that, and I'll change when you've finished. Think we can make it in forty-five minutes?'

'Of course.'

She disappeared into the bathroom to dress, emerging a few minutes later in a tracksuit and trainers, ready to drive Bess and the professor to hospital.

Driving was difficult. For the first time since her arrival on the island she was negotiating the narrow, cliff-hanging roads in the semi-dark of a northern summer night, in bad weather. She was also conscious of having on board a very ill patient in pain, as well as her own patient, the professor, under stress and nursing Bess in the back of the Range Rover. The fact that she had performed more hazardous journeys with wounded combatants during her spell with the WHO did little for her confidence.

Everyone said it was different when it was your own. How right they were, she reflected, pulling the steering-wheel round sharply to negotiate a particularly dramatic bend. Her concern was equally divided between the acutely ill Bess, and the chronically sick James.

Having young Jamie aboard was a mixed blessing. The knowledge that someone young and strong was on hand should anything untoward happen during their drive to the hospital was something of a comfort; but his nervous questions about his sister's condition were hard to deal with.

At last they arrived at the hospital, and Emma was thankful to hand over to the professional and experienced staff who greeted them on their arrival.

Because of James's status they were given VIP treatment, and invited to wait, while the operation was in progress, in the consultants' rest-room. Someone brought them coffee and sandwiches and told them to contact the reception desk should they wish for anything more.

In spite of the comfort of easy-chairs and food and drink, the time that Bess was in Theatre dragged. Emma and young Jamie kept looking surreptitiously at their watches, and turning towards the door whenever a sound penetrated from the corridor.

After a seemingly endless time the door opened, and Andrew Ffouldes, the consultant general surgeon who had come in especially to perform the operation on Bess, stood in the doorway.

'All over,' he said kindly, making his way towards James. 'Everything should be OK. I think she'll do, James, but it was a narrow squeak.'

James put out his hand and clasped that of his colleague. 'I can't thank you enough. Good of you to come in at this hour.' His voice was gruff, unlike his usual cool tones. He was no different from relatives of patients, faced with a life-threatening situation, Emma realised. All his training and expertise couldn't shield him from this overpowering emotional reaction to distress where a loved one was concerned.

'Glad to be of help,' answered Andrew Ffouldes with equal gruffness.

James, young Jamie and Emma all trooped in quietly to see Bess some time later. She was in the intensive care unit, with drips and tubes and monitors attached to her slender, quiet form. She was just conscious.

'Jamie,' she whispered to her brother, 'does Mummy know?'

Her brother shook his head. 'No, she had her tablets last night. She's still asleep. Uncle James and Nurse Emma have been looking after you.'

'Thank you,' murmured a pale and subdued Bess.

Both James and Emma muttered sympathetically, but didn't know how to deal with a child whose mother should have been there to comfort her. If, thought Emma, I'd had a little more time to get to know this child I might be more use to her. She bent over the hospital bed and kissed a pale cheek.

'Mummy will be here later,' she said with a reassuring smile.

# CHAPTER TEN

THE first few days following Bess's admission to hospital were difficult.

Nesta, from the outset, behaved badly. She first condemned them all, and poor Jamie in particular, for not waking her when Bess was taken ill. Jamie's protestations that Bess had tried to rouse her before going down to Nurse Emma made no impression on that lady. Even James's statement that they had tried to wake her before taking Bess to hospital failed to convince her that there wasn't some sort of conspiracy afoot.

Yet, when James told her that he had arranged for the hospital to give her a room for the period that Bess was in Intensive Care, she raised hell.

'I can't stay!' she said in a high, hysterical voice. 'I've got to meet someone in Rome the day after tomorrow.'

This extraordinary announcement occurred during the late breakfast that James, Jamie and Emma sat down to on their return from the hospital. Mrs Mac had managed to get Nesta up at some point, and she was sitting at the table nursing a cup of black coffee when they arrived home.

Everyone in the room turned astonished eyes on her.

'We're talking about your daughter, Nesta, the child you've just been castigating us about, complaining that we kept you in the dark,' James stated austerely.

Nesta looked wildly about her for a moment, then focused her attention on the professor.

'You don't understand!' she wailed. 'I don't want to leave Bess, but this is terribly important. James, I must speak to you in private. Now.' She pushed her chair noisily back from the table. 'Come,' she said imperiously. 'Somewhere where we won't be overheard.'

She started to stalk away from the table. James looked undecided for a moment. Emma put a hand on his arm.

'You've been up all night, James. Eat your breakfast and I'll attend to your eyes. Then you can shower and change, and then you can have a private conversation with Nesta, if she's prepared to wait that long before seeing Bess.'

Halfway to the door, Nesta turned.

'How dare you?' she spat out. 'You—you. . .'

'Nurse,' replied Emma in a steely voice. 'Because that's what I am, Mrs Leroux—a nurse. And I have a patient to care for—the professor. He, and only he, is my concern at this moment. I will not have his treatment disrupted any further.'

She wondered at her own temerity, facing up to this worldy, beautiful woman, who, even after a night's drugged sleep, looked marvellous. Whereas I, she thought, look a mess in a crumpled tracksuit, uncombed hair and no make-up. Just as well James can't see us and make a comparison.

It was James's voice that interrupted her thoughts.

'Emma's right, Nesta. I must have my treatment. She's the boss.' There was a sharp intake of breath from Nesta, who was on the point of saying more, when James stopped her. 'If you have any maternal feelings at all, my dear, you'll go and pack a case and be prepared to stay with Bess for the next few days.' He paused, looking infinitely weary. 'If you don't take this course of action I shall be forced to do something rather dramatic. I think you know what I mean.'

Jamie, who had been forgotten during this exchange, made a sobbing sound and rushed from the room, pushing his mother aside as he did so. 'You go to her,' he cried. 'She wants you.' And he fled, leaving the door swinging behind him.

'I can't,' called Nesta after him. 'I can't, Jamie, because of you and Bess.' She turned back to James. 'Help me,' she pleaded, on the verge of tears.

'When Emma has seen to my eyes,' he replied coldly, 'not before. Your hysterics will do for us all one day.'

He stood up and made for the treatment-room, and Emma followed. They didn't speak. Emma bathed and irrigated his eyes as usual and gave him the injection which was due. As she finished, James said, 'Sorry about all that, my dear. Nesta tends to get a bit het-up over things—red hair, I suppose.' He gave a strained smile. 'May I have your permission to speak to her before I shower and change, please?' He managed a smile.

'Perhaps you'd better, before she starts throwing things.' She tried to sound more light-hearted than she felt. 'I'll go and freshen up 'and come down and have the post ready for you later.' She moved to the door.

'Emma,' he said softly, 'thanks for everything. I'll find a way of proving how grateful I am some day.' He smiled again, this time more easily. 'Now, my love, will you ask Nesta to come to me here? This should be private enough for her.'

'Right away.'

* * *

Later Emma drove James and Jamie back from the hospital, where they had left a subdued Nesta, installed in a small room near Bess.

Only James and Nesta knew how matters had been resolved, for neither explained what had taken place in the treatment-room. Whatever had happened, though, he had persuaded Nesta to stay. Perhaps it had to do with the long telephone call that she made during the morning? Emma presumed that it was concerned in some way with the person she was to have met in Rome, as James asked her to get a Rome number after Nesta had finished her call. It was all very mysterious.

It's none of your business, she reminded herself, and set about planning a fresh programme of work, treatment and rest for James.

The arrival of Philippa and Angus, late on the evening after the emergency, helped. Surprisingly Philippa had her left arm in a sling.

'How stupid can you get?' she said, making a face. 'I tripped over a vacuum lead and produced a Colles'!' She pointed to her plastered wrist. 'Also gashed my knee. If it isn't presuming too much, Emma, may I ask you to include me in your treatment session in the morning, and renew the dressing?'

Emma agreed happily. It would be great to have a little more basic nursing to do.

'She only did it to get some time off,' said Angus in a typically heartless brotherly fashion.

'I'm still very capable, little brother,' Philippa replied with a laugh, 'of doing you real damage with my good hand!'

It was lovely to have them there, laughing and joking and obviously pleasing James with their banter. They appreciated, too, the strain that he and Emma had been under since Nesta's arrival.

'Anything we can do,' they said in unison.

'I'm sorry,' said James when they had finished supper and retired to the sitting-room, 'that it won't be the sort of break you both deserve and must have been looking forward to. But Emma and I would be grateful if you'd share the visits to the cottage hospital and driving for a day or two.'

'Well,' replied Angus, pouring everyone a good measure of James's best malt, 'I consider a few visits and a bit of driving small repayment for some of Mackie's superb meals.'

'I second that, though I won't be much use on the driving front,' confirmed Philippa, raising her glass in a gesture of praise to the absent Mrs Mac. She turned to Emma. 'And a vote of thanks to you too, Emma. I don't know what James would have done without you.'

Emma blushed and murmured incoherently. James grinned and said that he thought she had been, 'Bloody marvellous.'

'You know,' he continued, 'she not only sorted Bess out, but got Jamie to co-operate. And that takes some doing.'

'I'm tired,' said Emma suddenly, unable to take more praise, not entirely sure it was genuine, half convinced that he was just being kind. 'If you don't mind, I'll go to bed now.'

'Must you?' asked James.

'Yes,' she replied firmly, 'I must.'

Sleep did not come readily, as it should have done, considering the long day and sleepless night preceding it. Emma tossed and turned, trying to sort out the strange relationship that existed between James and Nesta. She was angry on behalf of Bess and Jamie, who seemed to be at times neglected by their mother, at times over-indulged by her.

It seemed incredible that Nesta hadn't wanted to go immediately to Bess's bedside, or to stay with her. Whatever could be more important than being with one's own sick child? And what had she meant by the remark she had made to Jamie about its being because of *them* that she had to go to Rome?

Who was the person Nesta had to see who was so important that he or she took precedence over Bess's need? Someone, moreover, whom she seemed afraid of offending if she didn't turn up on time. It was almost as if she felt threatened by that person. Everything connected with Mrs Leroux seemed slightly strange and sinister.

At last Emma fell into an uneasy sleep, from which she awoke in the morning unrefreshed. Worries rushed in on her. She felt anxious on James's behalf. He must be persuaded to rest a little more today to make up for the recent physical and emotional turmoil. She hoped he wouldn't be difficult about it, and was cheered by the knowledge that his brother and sister were there to back her up.

In spite of her bad night she had woken early, according to her custom. No one was about when she went downstairs. It was still dull, as it had been the day before, but the wild wind and occasional outbursts of rain had ceased, and the temperature had risen again to a tropical, humid heat.

She decided to go for a swim, and went into the cubicle and shower area near the terrace door. She had left a bikini drying in there after an evening swim, and it ought to still be around. Sure enough, it was there with the usual pile of fresh, fluffy towels that Mrs Mac regularly checked.

Emma changed quickly, slipping into the brief suit that made it feel as if she was almost swimming in the nude, and ran down the path and across the sandy shore to the sea. The water was colder than it had been on her last swim. It made her gasp as she dipped her warm body beneath the surface. But it soothed and stimulated at the same time. What a pity that James wasn't here to appreciate the calming effect of the still, though grey, waters.

His voice hailed her from the shore. He was near the rocky outcrop, clad in brief black trunks, not the boxer shorts that he had previously worn. He had shed his double shield from his eyes and was minus his dark glasses, but had a small waterproof protective covering over his recently infected eye, as well as a pair of swimming goggles. As one would have expected, he was doing all the right things.

'Come out and join me on the raft,' Emma called.

He was with her in a few minutes, diminishing the distance from the shore with a strong breast-stroke. He clambered on to the wooden raft.

'Two minds,' he said, giving her one of his most devastating smiles. 'Somehow I thought I'd find you swimming.'

'Why?'

'I'm not sure. It's just that I seem to be on the same wavelength as you.' He dropped his voice to a deeper tone. 'You do things to me, Emma. I've never felt like this about anyone before. Do you know, there's an old song which says something about being past love?'

Emma shook her head. 'No, I don't know that one.'

'Well, the gist of it is that, when you think you're past love, you discover the real thing. I'm crashing forty, dearest girl, and have had a few false alarms where love is concerned, but,' he put an arm round her shoulder, 'that's how I feel about you. I've found my last love, and I should like to make you my only love.'

A mild shaft of sunshine penetrated the grey clouds. It was surprisingly warm. The sea in an instant changed from grey to pale green, lit with patches of gold where the rays of sun hit the surface of a wave.

Emma thought, It's rather like my feelings, sparked to life by a few words from James. She looked at the man she loved, sitting hunched beside her on the raft, the patch over one eye making him look rakish and rather piratical. His thick black hair was moulded against his head, the white streak, magpie-like, a brush-stroke from widow's peak to the pointed cluster of curls at the nape of his neck.

'Your hair needs cutting,' she said in a matter-of-fact voice.

He gave a shout of delighted laughter.

'Darling, you're priceless,' he said. 'Here am I, laying my heart at your feet, practically proposing, and you say that my hair needs cutting.'

'Well, it does.' No way was she going to let him know of the tumult that was raging inside her at his words. One of us, she thought, must keep our head, and, since he's my patient, it had better be me.

She sidled a little away from him, a move that was frustrated as the raft tilted first one way and then the other, and she slipped back even closer to him than before. He cradled her in his arms.

'My dear and lovely Emma, please don't move away from me again. I meant what I said, you know, and if we hadn't had so many appalling interruptions over the last few days I would have declared myself before.'

She said shakily, 'James, we hardly know each other. Please don't rush me.'

'Oh, yes, we do,' he replied firmly. 'Know each other, I mean. That's what falling in love is all about, my dearest. You always know everything about the loved one. It doesn't mean to say that there's nothing wrong with the person one loves—one perceives it, but chooses to accept or ignore it. Love isn't blind, it's quite the opposite, but it's selective.'

Emma felt that the only way she could deal with his declaration was to diminish it by making gentle fun of them both.

'What must we look like,' she said, determinedly cheerful, 'sitting on a raft in the middle of Skye philosophising about love?'

'Well, I don't know how I look, my love, but you look stunning—a silver mermaid.' He touched the flimsy white material of the tiny top of her bikini.

'Oh, no,' she said, in a flash knowing that if he touched her with any intimacy she would be lost. All common sense would go. She would find herself agreeing to whatever he suggested.

Somehow she wriggled from his arms and slipped over the side of the raft.

'Beat you to the shore,' she called over her shoulder as she struck out and swam like mad.

James overtook her within a minute or so, cruising up beside her as she made strenuous efforts to stay in front.

'One of the few things,' he said softly, 'that I can perhaps beat you at is swimming. I've spent half my life in water!'

Emma snorted, but only succeeded in swallowing a huge mouthful of water. She was still coughing and spluttering when they reached the beach.

'Want any help?' asked James.

'No, thank you,' she retorted, flinging a towel about her shoulders with as much dignity as she could muster as she marched towards the house.

She heard him laugh in a quiet, confident manner. Beast, she thought, he knows just how I feel. I haven't got a chance of fighting him off while we're both here together.

But her heart wasn't in her pretended rejection of him. With all her being she wanted what he was offering: his love, protection, strength. For, in spite of his present disabilities, he was strength personified. Not just in the purely physical manner that he had just illustrated by overtaking her on the swim back to the shore, but in his intellectual and emotional responses to her.

He truly believed in an equality of ability. When he talked about his work as a plastic surgeon he always spoke of team effort. Everyone in Theatre, and afterwards in Intensive Care and the wards, he insisted, was part of the team. They all contributed to the patients' return to health, and not one of the team, from himself, as senior surgeon, down to the humblest nurse, could function without the help of the others. If there were only more men of intelligence and power around, the cause of women's rights and equality might be more advanced.

These thoughts, and many more, surged through Emma's head as she showered and dressed for the day. Later, when they met at breakfast, she was able to put on a calm, cheerful face, quelling her tumultuous

thoughts, which was just as well, as both Philippa and
Angus were present. Later they were joined by a
subdued Jamie, who wanted to know how soon somebody was going to take him in to see Bess.

'I will,' volunteered a cheerful Angus, 'as soon as
I've finished breakfast.'

Jamie looked at him suspiciously. 'You won't try to
rush me away, will you?' he asked. 'I want to spend a
long time with Bess.'

Angus looked a bit shattered. 'How do you mean, a
long time?'

'Well, most of the day, really.'

Emma intervened. 'Look, Angus, after you've seen
Bess, why don't you come back, and I'll drive over
later this afternoon to collect Jamie? I can look in on
Bess too.'

'Good idea,' said James. 'We can both go.'

'I thought we were supposed to be saving you two
from too many visits,' said Philippa in a practical voice.

'Well, there's not so much pressure now, is there,
Emma?' James had resumed wearing his dark glasses
and had to turn his head to see her even faintly.

She thought there was a double meaning to his
words, but couldn't be sure. 'No,' she said quietly. 'It's
marvellous to have support.'

'Then that's settled,' said James happily, and even
young Jamie seemed satisfied.

Emma's treatment-room was rather like a miniature
Out-patients that morning. Philippa came in, having
asked permission from Emma to watch while James
was receiving his treatment. Then she sat in the chair
and exposed her gashed leg, while James stood leaning
against the wall as Emma attended to his sister.

Emma's first remark when she saw the long tear in Philippa's leg expressed her surprise.

'Why on earth wasn't this stitched?' she asked. 'It should have been. I can't believe that any casualty officer would have let you go without stitching.'

Philippa looked embarrassed. 'That's my fault, I'm afraid,' she said. 'I didn't mention my leg, or rather I said it was only a scratch when I reported the accident. I'm afraid the junior casualty officer on duty rather took my word for it.' She asked, sounding rather anxious, 'Do you think that it's bad enough to need stitching, Emma?'

'Yes, I do, and it wasn't very fair to the young houseman not to let him look at it.'

Philippa looked even more embarrassed. 'Yes, you're quite right, it wasn't fair. But I honestly thought that it wasn't much of an injury. I was wearing well-fitting tights, and there didn't seem to be much bleed-,ing. What do you suggest, Emma?'

'That James has a go.'

'Dear girl!' exclaimed James, taken quite by surprise. 'Will you let me?'

Emma grinned. For the first time in days she felt in control of things. It was rather ironic that these two superbly qualified doctors should be depending on her advice. 'Well, you're allowed some time without your shield, and one eye is functioning near-perfectly, so I don't see any reason why you, as the best stitcher around, shouldn't perform this small service for your sister; that is, of course, if she's prepared to risk it.'

The pleasure that James showed in her suggestion made up for her boldness and minuscule doubts as to his ability to perform what would normally be an ordinary task beneath his expert fingers. But he hadn't worked for several months, and his one eye, though working well, was not the same as having the use of two perfectly sighted eyes. Nor could they, on account of his fatigue syndrome, be absolutely certain that his hitherto superbly performing fingers would respond to the demands made upon them.

It was really up to Philippa.

'James,' she said throatily, 'I'd be eternally grateful if you would perform the minor miracle of stitching me up without too much distortion. You know how it can be. A bad scar and a constant reminder that one's legs were not what one hoped that they would be.'

'I certainly do understand, sister dear,' he said with a nice smile. 'Half my female and most of my male patients are concerned about the after-effects of treatment. I'll do my best, Philly, to make you presentable on the beach in a bikini.'

'So be it. Emma, will you set up a tray for big brother, please?'

'Of course.'

It took James a long time to stitch his sister's leg. This was partly because a few days had passed since the original injury, and partly because he was very concerned to bring the external skin together to leave the minimum of scarring. It was the neatest repair job that Emma had ever seen. He quite clearly had not lost his touch. She put cicatrin powder and a clean dry dressing over the wound.

'Go and have coffee,' she suggested. 'I'll be with you shortly after I've tidied in here.'

'OK, Bossy Boots,' said James, sounding incredibly happy. 'But don't be long, my love.'

The endearment caused Philippa to raise surprised eyebrows, but James was oblivious to this. Obviously, doing what he would normally have considered a very mundane piece of medical work had cheered him no end.

It must be good for him to get back to some kind of work, mused Emma as she tidied, sterilised and reset her treatment trolley for the evening session.

If James had thought that the evening drive to the hospital would give him and Emma time alone together he was doomed to be frustrated.

'I'd like to come, if I may,' said Philippa just as they were about to leave. 'I should look in on Bess and, I suppose, say a word to Nesta.'

It was clearly much more of a duty visit than a desire on Philippa's part to see the invalid or her mother. Emma was rather surprised that James's clever sister hadn't sensed his feelings and realised that he would like to be alone with his nurse.

No such lack of intuition or feelings had inhibited Angus, though it was not until the third day after his arrival that he mentioned it.

He joined Emma early that morning when she was preparing to go swimming.

'It's all right,' he said in a kind and friendly manner. 'I just wanted to let you know that I can see how things are between you and James. I don't want to butt in, but, should you ever want a shoulder to cry on, I'm available. I know my big brother.'

He plunged into the water and swam a long way out into the bay before she could question him. What had he meant about James when he'd said that he knew about his 'big brother'? It was almost as if he expected him to let her down!

She had purposely avoided visiting the beach before

breakfast since the morning that James had seemed to declare his love for her. He had not sought her out since then, or since that evening when Philippa had unexpectedly joined them on their visit to the hospital. Emma had no idea if he was avoiding her. Perhaps, she thought, he regretted his impulsive actions on the raft? Was that what Angus had meant?

Of course, they met daily, at mealtimes, and in the course of her duties in the treatment-room, where she now also inspected Philippa's leg from time to time. In addition, they were together when he was dictating or examining tapes and records for his book. But there was now a subtle difference: he was less dependent upon her. He could read the post for himself, and attend to much of the written work contained in his notes. Both Dr MacLeod, in person, and Sir Hugh Robertson, by phone and letter, had given permission for him to discard his protective specs for much of the day.

So the days passed with their seeing each other, but seldom being alone together, except when working. It was a strange, uncomfortable time, with both of them trying to behave normally, yet aware that matters weren't normal between them.

It was just over a week after Bess had been admitted to hospital that the matron telephoned to say that Mrs Leroux had left. Later that day Nesta phoned from somewhere *en route*, to say that she was going to Rome.

Whatever he felt about the matter, James didn't reveal anything. But he turned to Emma as he put down the phone.

'Would you be prepared to take on looking after

Bess as she convalesces?' he asked. 'I don't fancy leaving her at the hospital without constant visiting, and, with Angus now gone and Philippa still barred from driving, it's going to be difficult.'

'No problem; I'll love looking after her.'

'Thank you, dear girl.'

He moved towards her very quickly over the polished floor of the sitting-room, and she was in his arms before she realised his intentions.

'James, don't—oh, please don't!'

He kept his arms round her. 'You've been avoiding me, my love, for the past week or so, and I've tried to respect your feelings, and held off, but I honestly don't think that I can any longer. Please, love, say you'll think about what I said that morning on the raft. I meant every word. My feelings haven't changed one bit.'

'Did you mean it?' she asked, recalling Angus's words. 'Really mean it?'

'I was asking you to marry me then, Emma, and I'm repeating the offer. I love you, my dear, more than life itself. And, if that sounds rather far-fetched, please remember that I've not too recently been in danger of losing the precious commodity of life.'

Emma found herself fumbling for words.

'Time,' she said. 'I need time. I don't expect you to understand, James, but I must know that you really want me. Not just as a nurse, a secretary, a general helpmate, but for me myself.' She was aware as she spoke that her words might sound odd, as if she was questioning his motives. In all honesty she had to admit that she was. Angus's words had shaken her. The idea that James might be human enough to make rash promises was shattering.

James slightly relaxed his hold on her and looked down into her upturned face.

He cupped her chin with one hand.

'The last thing I want,' he said, 'is to push you into something you're not sure of. I have this feeling that we belong together, and I believe you share that feeling. For some reason you don't want to acknowledge it. You would, of course, be entitled to consider the difference in our ages a barrier. If you remember, my love, I suggested this myself.'

Emma looked at him in astonishment.

'Good lord, of course I don't think that matters. It has nothing to do with how I feel. It's just that. . .'

She couldn't go on. How to explain that she wasn't sure she would be able to live up to him and his social scene, even if she was able to accept his offer of marriage as honestly made. His age as such was no barrier, but probably his friends were, in the main, more his age than hers. She hadn't thought of that before. Could this be a problem? And maybe his ideas of marriage were rather different from her own, though quite how she didn't know.

He'd spoken half jokingly, she'd thought, about finding his last love. Now she wondered, for all her earlier certainty that he was the one and only man in her life, if her love was as strong as his seemed to be. She still felt hopelessly attracted to him, but was this because of their nurse-patient relationship, and his calm maturity? Had it to do with the romantic aura of the island of Skye, steeped in a history of brave deeds and kilted clansmen and a Stuart prince?

James had worn a kilt once or twice when they had visited friends for the evening, and he had looked stunning—more handsome than any other man in the room. Had all this contributed to her feelings for him? Perhaps his age had made an appeal to her need to be cared for? Perhaps her motives rather than his needed scrutiny? Perhaps, perhaps. . .

Panic swamped her. There seemed to be no end of questions, and no answers to any of them. To her horror she realised that tears were trickling down her cheeks.

'Here, what's all this?' James brushed the tears away with gentle fingers. He cradled her gently in his arms until she stopped crying, then gave her a gentle push. 'Go on, love,' he said. 'Go and wash your face and make yourself even more beautiful, and we'll away to fetch young Bess home.'

# CHAPTER ELEVEN

WITH three people to attend to, Emma was busy. She treated James and Philippa each morning before going up to see Bess. The child's progress was slow due to a wound infection, though she felt, in herself, ready for anything.

'You'll soon be fit,' consoled Emma one morning after changing the dressing over the slowly healing scar.

Emma still found it strange that Jamie and Bess seemed to accept their mother's departure so calmly. Now that Bess was out of danger, neither she nor Jamie appeared to need Nesta.

It was all part of the cosmopolitan life that the MacDonalds and their friends lived, she supposed. The way of life that she, in her parochial fashion, found hard to come to terms with. The lifestyle that made a long-term future with James seem unlikely. . .

A week after Bess's return to the Old House Philippa, spending ages on the phone, convinced her chief at her London hospital that she could be useful with one hand, and returned there the following day.

'At last,' said James fervently, 'we can get back to some sort of normality.'

He and Emma were driving back from Mallaig, where they had seen Philippa safely on board the ferry. Emma felt elated. He was obviously pleased that the last of their visitors, excluding the twins, had gone. In a way, these days, Jamie and Bess hardly counted as visitors. Jamie was delighted to have his sister home, and spent hours with her. They remained, for the most part, locked in a close and mutual understanding with each other, but they were less sullen than they had been when they had arrived. It was quite true what James had said: freed of their mother's presence, they responded to normal adult company without rebellion. They slotted into the household like chameleons, causing hardly a ripple in the domestic and working arrangements of the house.

With Philippa's departure, the weather changed. The hot, sunny spell that had enhanced her last few days on the island broke. A fierce storm was building as James and Emma made their way home from Mallaig. The wind strengthened, rocking their car. Mountainous seas and Cinemascope-type lightning flashed across the bay and illuminated the Cuillins beyond.

'Heaven help the fisher-folk on a night like this,' said Mrs Mac as she greeted them at the door and relieved them of their coats, soaked in the short run from the car. 'Now, the bairns are having their supper upstairs, and your meal will be ready in half an hour in the dining-room.'

James and Emma arrived in the sitting-room together after showering and changing ready for dinner.

'This is very civilised,' said James, eyeing her mid-calf-length black silk skirt and soft rose-coloured cashmere sweater, which she had decided was just right for a chilly summer evening. 'You look delightful, my dear. Now, will you have your usual?'

'Please.'

With only one eye covered he was able to dispense their dry Martinis with ease. They sat drinking them at the picture-windows overlooking the turbulent bay. The ice clinked in a satisfactory manner in their glasses. James looked more relaxed than she had seen him for weeks. Emma smiled quietly to herself. Now, she thought, he has a real chance of recovery from his damaged eye and his fatigue syndrome.

'A penny for them,' he said. 'The happy thoughts that are making you smile.'

'Oh, I'd forgotten that you can see.' Emma smiled directly at him. 'I was just thinking that you'll have time and opportunity now to resume your "get well" programme.'

Mrs Mac came in and announced that dinner was ready. It was a beautiful meal—leek and potato soup, chicken breasts, salad and new potatoes, followed by a steaming blackcurrent sponge and cream. They took their coffee into the sitting-room.

James said softly, 'Shall we try a duet? The last time we played together was with a third party present.'

'I'd like that.'

They sat side by side at the piano for nearly an hour, 'murdering', so James said, Schubert, Liszt and Mozart. Then they went modern with Scott Joplin and Andrew Lloyd Webber. Their physical nearness was enhanced by their musical awareness, fingers rapidly caressing the keys in a wonderful bonding of sensuality and enjoyment.

The music seemed to bring them together as nothing else had. They were satiated with it.

James took Emma into his arms at the end of the evening, but it was a tender, gentle embrace, free from sexual overtones.

'One day,' he said huskily, 'it will come right— everything will come right.'

They parted at the top of the stairs, he to his room, she to hers.

In spite of the wind and rain battering at the windows, Emma fell asleep almost as soon as her head touched the pillow. She felt warm, comforted and unthreatened by James's action earlier in the evening. She had rather expected, with his brother and sister both off the premises, that he might make a more direct approach. The fact that he hadn't presumed on their absence to press his cause made her feel protected, less vulnerable.

It was at one-thirty in the morning that she became aware of first several loud bangs, like gunshot in the distance, and then a hammering on her door.

'Come in,' she called, and young Jamie almost fell through the door, followed by a shaky Bess.

'Here,' said Emma at once, thinking Bess was in trouble, 'hop in.' She pulled the bedclothes back from the other side of the bed.

'No,' said Bess loudly, 'I'm all right. It's a boat, in the bay, in trouble.'

James, looking as always elegant, appeared in the doorway, pulling on a silk dressing-gown over pyjamas.

'What is it?' he asked.

The twins turned to him in obvious relief, and briefly Emma wondered why they had come to her when they might have alerted their godfather.

'It's a boat,' they said in unison, 'in the bay, in trouble. They've sent up maroons.'

'Right, let's get down there. But not you, Bess—sorry, but you're not up to it. Look, you try contacting the rescue services direct—the number's on the board above the phone in the study. Then wake up Mrs Mac, if she's not up already, and let her know what's happening.' He turned towards his room. 'We'd better get dressed,' he said, indicating himself, Emma and Jamie.

Emma put on a tracksuit and running shoes and went downstairs to the cloakroom and put on her mac. James and Jamie were already there, similarly attired and armed with torches and coils of rope. James handed her a torch.

'We'll put on all the outside lights,' he said, 'and, should the power go, you, Jamie, will start up the generator. Remember how to get it going?'

'Course I do!'

'Right, Emma, bring the surgery bag, will you, please, just in case?'

It was quite frightening, stepping out from the terrace into the teeth of the storm. The night was pitch-black, lit every few seconds by great flashes of lightning which illuminated the huge waves crashing on the beach. Thunder cracked and roared seemingly from every direction, and the rain sheeted down in one continuous stream.

As they made their way down to the shore a rocket pierced the inky blackness, scattering a shower of stars just above the rowan tree.

'Thank God she's not too far out,' shouted James. 'We might be able to get to her from the rocks.' He called something else over his shoulder, but his words were flung away in the wind and lost as thunder bellowed overhead.

Another blinding flash of lightning threw the boat into relief for a moment. It was half on its side and one of its two masts was broken and lying across the sloping deck. As they got nearer they could see a light bobbing about and hear the ragged remnants of voices calling.

Both James and Jamie shouted back. Emma was too breathless with battling against the wind and rain to shout. She waved her torch in the direction of the wrecked vessel, hoping it would be seen by those on board, and give them some comfort.

Once they were on the outcrop the full force of the storm hit them. Mingled with the relentless rain was spray shooting high above their heads in great plumes as it hit the rocks. James bent to shout instructions to Emma and Jamie.

'I'm going to tie one end of the rope to the tree, and the other round my waist. There are only a few feet of water between us and the boat. Keep your torches on me, and if you think I'm in difficulties haul me back if you can. When I'm on deck I'll flash my torch twice. That'll be the signal for you to come aboard, Jamie. Understand?' Somehow he managed a rather grim smile. Jamie nodded. James looked at Emma. 'You stay here, Emma, and wait for a message. Hang on to the bag; I might want it later.'

She wanted to stop him from plunging into the foaming sea, but knew that she couldn't. Nothing would stop him.

She nodded that she understood. James took off his mac before lowering himself into the boiling waters; obviously it would get in the way. I must remember that, Emma thought incongruously, if I have to go on board. It was amazing how calmly she considered the possibility.

She and Jamie watched James's torch, which he held high above his head, move steadily towards the ship's side. The light wavered and arced, distorted by rain and spray.

'How will he get on board?' Emma shrieked at Jamie. 'It looks so high in the water.'

'Someone'll give him a hand. He'll be OK,' answered Jamie, sounding very confident. 'He knows about boats.'

Yes, of course he does, she thought. He'd told her that day on the raft that he was used to swimming and anything to do with the sea.

By shining both their torches across the narrow stretch of water they were able to see James when he reached the boat, being helped aboard by two shadowy figures. Almost at once he turned and flashed his torch for Jamie to join him.

He yelled something, but they couldn't hear. Then one word emerged as he called again: 'Case!'

'He wants me to take the surgical case across,' said Jamie.

'But you can't—it'll get wet.'

'No, it won't. The water was only up to Uncle's waist. I'm tall enough to keep it dry if I hold it above my head,' yelled Jamie.

Emma capitulated. She really had no choice. Obviously James had been told of someone in need of attention immediately he'd got on board, and he needed the medication that was in the case.

Jamie did exactly as James had done. He took off his mac and tied one end of his rope round his waist and the other to the tree. They had seen James fasten his rope to a rail on the deck of the boat, so Jamie had a guide-line of sorts.

'The same signal with the torch—two flashes if

you're needed,' he said. 'I'll come back for you or send my rope over.'

Emma nodded and handed him the case, which he balanced, supported with one hand, on top of his head. In the other hand he held his torch and grasped the rope that James had attached to the boat.

'Be careful, Jamie,' said Emma, holding the rope and going with him to the edge of the rocks.

'Thanks,' he said, and smiled as he clambered down into the water—the first smile that he'd given her.

It seemed a long time after she had seen Jamie helped aboard the boat that anyone tried to make contact with her. She stood on the rocky outcrop beneath the rowan tree, battered by the rain and wind and spray, feeling lonely and helpless. That was the worst feature of waiting, in fact—feeling useless. There had to be a medical emergency aboard for James to have needed the case immediately. She had a strong feeling that she should be there in such an emergency. She wasn't and that was difficult to accept.

After what seemed an age, Jamie appeared again on the dangerously sloping deck, together with another person.

'We're coming over!' he shouted in his loud boy's voice, beating the roar of wind and waves. Emma saw him fix the rope, which he had secured to the boat earlier, round himself and his companion. They slid from the tilted deck into the water. She took hold of the rope a yard or so from the tree and heaved. She could feel the weight on the end of the rope, and pulled again, hoping that it was helping Jamie and his companion, glad to be doing something.

At last, breathless with their efforts, Jamie and

another boy of about his age clambered up the slippery rocks.

'Uncle James wants you to go over and help him,' said Jamie. 'One of the crew has a broken leg, a below-knee fracture, he said, and somebody else is concussed—I think that's the word he used.' He looked at his companion for confirmation.

The other boy nodded. 'My dad,' he said.

Now that the moment had come for her to be useful Emma found that she had to call up all her courage to begin the short journey from shore to vessel. Like Jamie, she did everything that James had done, and then, with the rope securely about her waist, slid into the cold green water. The tide nearly swept her off her feet, but she reasoned that, though much shorter than James, she was as tall as Jamie, and he had made it. Her light weight was against her, but at last she fetched up against the side of the boat.

This was her worst moment. The deck, at an even sharper angle than it had appeared from the shore, reared above her. There was no one around. She clung to a little protruding rail and shouted as hard as she could. After what seemed an age, but was probably only seconds, a waterproofed figure appeared above her.

'Give me your hand!' he yelled to make himself heard above the elements.

Reluctantly Emma removed one hand from the railing and he grabbed it urgently.

'Heave,' he said, and, suiting actions to words, dragged her from the water. Her arms felt as if they were being pulled from their sockets. She landed on the slippery boards in a wet heap, clawing at anything to give her the purchase that would prevent her sliding back into the water.

The man hauled her to her feet. 'The doc wants you in the cabin.' He pushed her towards the short flight of steps that led downwards at an unlikely angle.

Somehow she made it, though she slid rather than walked down the last few steps.

James looked up as she entered. 'Emma—good, you're here,' he said briskly as if they were doing a ward-round. 'We'll have to make up splints for this man—definitely a fracture of tib and fib, and possible damage to femur. See what you can find.'

She felt a stab of resentment at James's indifference to her bedraggled appearance and the effort she had made to join him, then realised that she was being ridiculous and unprofessional.

She ferreted around in the cupboards and came up with a broom, from which she removed the brush head.

'Great, that'll do for the outside leg—now something shorter if possible for a below-knee splint.'

The man who had helped her on deck pulled back the cushions of a long narrow bench, tilted, as everything else, at a perilous angle.

'One of these any good?' he asked, pulling a flat support strip from the framework.

'Fine.'

James had already given an injection of pethidine to the injured man to kill the pain. He rambled incoherently, mercifully only partly aware of what was happening. They secured the long broom handle to the outside of the injured leg from ankle to hip, and the short flat piece of wood between his legs from knee to ankle. To supplement the bandages and pads from the surgical case, Emma tore strips from the curtains at the small cabin windows.

It was awkward attending to the patient on the sloping floor; they had to crouch in a half-sitting, half-kneeling position. The cabin was not very large, and the man with the head injury that the boys had mentioned was lying in a cramped position between the cabin and what was apparently the galley.

'I've done what I can for him pro tem,' said James, indicating the unconscious man as they finished tying the last pad in place on the fracture patient. 'He's as warm and comfortable as we can make him. His pupils are equal and he seems not to be too deeply concussed, but, of course, he'll need to be looked at properly when we get ashore. According to Matt here,' he nodded towards the uninjured crewman, 'he slipped as the boat turned over and cracked his head against the door frame.'

'That's right,' confirmed Matt, giving them a shaky grin. 'It's poor old Robert here who really caught it. He was on deck when the mast came down. Trevor and I managed with young Terry's help to get him in here, and just after that Trev got knocked out. The kid was bloody marvellous.'

'Well, now we've got to think about getting ashore,' said James, 'but we'll hang on a bit. With luck the emergency services will be here soon. They'll organise our return trip.' He gave both Emma and Matt a rather distant and tired smile.

Emma offered up a silent prayer that he was right. The idea of making the journey back to the shore with two injured men was horrendous. It was going to be bad enough screwing up her courage to wade back through the icy water herself, without the added problems of helpless patients to contend with.

She was also beginning to worry about James now that the initial crisis of dealing with the fractured leg and concussed patient was over. He was still high on adrenalin at present, but at what point would his diminished resources begin to affect him, and how would that affect his eyesight and fatigue syndrome?

The three of them carried on a desultory conversation while they waited, though James seemed rather remote. Matt went up on deck a couple of times to see if anyone had arrived, but came back with a negative shake of his head each time.

'But the boys are still there,' he said. 'Young Terry won't go till his dad's ashore, and your boy insists that he might be needed. At least the rain and wind have died down.'

'Right, we'll give the services another ten minutes, and if they're not here by then I'll send the boys to the house for news, and hot drinks. They must be wretchedly cold and uncomfortable by now. At least we're reasonably dry in here,' James said in a colourless voice.

About five minutes later there was a piercing whistle from outside, and when they went up on deck they found that both the police and an ambulance had arrived.

With the weather conditions improved and four large men used to dealing with inert bodies at work, the injured were transferred ashore safely. Matt and Terry were offered accommodation in the Old House for the night, but refused. They accepted the offer of the police officers to take them to the hospital, staying just long enough to get into dry clothes and have hot drinks and sandwiches prepared by Mrs Mac and Bess.

James, young Jamie and Emma also went off to change into dry clothes, but they were still all too excited by the night's events to go to bed. They met up in the sitting-room to hold a post-mortem on the unexpected adventure.

It was a pleasure to see Bess and Jamie really behaving like children for once; exaggerating what had happened, trying to make it sound even more adventurous, and appealing to James and, surprisingly, to Emma for support.

She and James sat side by side on the long sofa sipping brandy, which he had prescribed as a nightcap. After a while he flung his arm casually along the back of the sofa and rested his hand on her shoulder, which he squeezed gently. Then he moved closer to her so that their hips and thighs were touching. His nearness produced an exquisite sensation, and she was unable to stop herself trembling.

For a moment nobody was taking any notice of them. They might have been alone. The children, across the other side of the room, were arguing noisily and Mrs Mac was adjudicating.

James murmured close to her ear, 'You were wonderful tonight, love. You must have been terrified crossing the water—I know I damn well was. And when you arrived on board all I could do was bite your head off! But I was sick with anxiety for you, afraid that you'd be washed away and I should lose you forever. My imagination worked overtime.'

'So did mine, I was scared for you too, James.'

'Were you?' He sounded surprised. 'You looked so calm and collected, very ward sisterish! Producing splints at the drop of a hat, carrying on a conversation with that fellow Matt about where he and his mates had been sailing. . .' He saw the look on her face. 'Oh, I know, love, you were just doing your Florence Nightingale bit and trying to take his mind off things. But would you believe I resented the fact?'

Emma chuckled. 'I thought you sounded just like a consultant doing a round, looking down your nose very haughtily. You terrified me.'

'Never,' he said incredulously.

They stared at each other, their eyes locked together. James's hand tightened on her shoulder till it hurt.

'Oh, my dearest love,' he whispered.

At that moment Bess and Jamie came across the room. 'Mrs Mac says that we've to go to bed, so we've come to say goodnight.'

Somehow James and Emma dragged their eyes away from each other and made suitable replies to the children.

At the doorway, Mrs Mac turned. 'And you two had better be away to your beds the while,' she said in her soft Highland voice. 'The boat people will be here to look at the vessel in an hour or so, and ye need some sleep, the pair of you.'

James gathered Emma into his arms when they had gone. He kissed her gently—butterfly kisses, brushing his lips over her cheeks and eyelids, and down her slender throat. He unfastened the warm soft top of the jump-suit that she'd put on when she'd changed from her wet clothes, and parted the front.

'Oh, my darling, you're beautiful. I want you so much.' He bent his head, and his lips touched her naked breasts and his tongue teased her nipples till they were taut with desire.

She moaned with pleasure, and pushed her hands through his thick black and white hair. He raised his head and looked searchingly at her. Since he no longer had to wear a protecting shield at night, he surveyed her with both piercing dark eyes, and saw that her eyes were full of love and longing.

'You're sure, my love?' he asked, his voice thick and heavy with pent-up emotion.

'Please—oh, yes, please!'

He smiled a smile that took her breath away and heightened her already receptive senses. She gave a great shuddering sigh as he slowly, with expert hands, eased the suit down over her hips, and off. It seemed to Emma that he did everything in slow motion, gently moving her from his lap till she was lying on the sofa and he was kneeling beside it, covering her naked body with kisses.

He stood up and stripped off his clothes before he lowered himself on to her.

Everything about their coming together was as near perfect as it could be. He was a gentle and considerate lover.

At last they fell asleep in each other's arms, covered by a tartan rug that he'd fetched from the cloaks cupboard.

They were awakened by a crash from the kitchen.

'Bloody hell—it's past eight o'clock!' said James. He produced a sleepy smile and a kiss to go with it. 'That, if I'm not mistaken, is Oona, letting the world and his wife know that she's arrived for work.' He gave Emma a prod. 'Away with ye, hussy, before you destroy my reputation altogether!' He grinned. 'Unless, of course, you want to brazen it out, my darling. Here, let me help you.' He picked up her suit from the floor. 'Jump in, love.' Then, suddenly very tender, he asked, 'Was it good for you too?'

Emma nodded. 'I didn't realise that making love could be like that. Thank you.'

James was serious. 'Thank you, my darling, for everything. We must talk soon, get things sorted out. Now, away with you, dear heart.' He kissed her in a positive, satisfactory manner and steered her to the bottom of the stairs.

When she looked down from the landing he was still there, draped in the tartan rug that had covered them during the few hours that they'd spent on the sofa.

# CHAPTER TWELVE

EMMA stood on the top of the Scott Monument looking down on one of the most famous views in the world. Far below lay Princes Street, stretching across the busy centre of Edinburgh. From this height it looked like a long, narrow, straight ribbon swarming with squat foreshortened people and toy motor cars.

She gazed out over the beautiful city, seeing but not taking in the wonderful view. Her mind and heart were back at the hospital with James.

It was four days since the night of the storm and two days since she'd noted, with horror, slight inflammation round his eyes.

She had asked calmly, as she often did, 'How do they feel this morning, James?'

'Fine, darling girl, thanks to you.' He was inclined to be amorous, his lips curled into the sensuous smile that she loved. He stretched out a hand to touch her.

'James, behave yourself!' She pretended to be cross to hide her concern while she found words to tell him what she had discovered. It would be a dreadful blow, just when everything seemed to be going along so well—a backward step, with unknown consequences. Of course, it might be just a mild set-back, she reassured herself. There was no reason to fear the worst, but her heart plummeted.

In spite of her quiet professionalism, he was suddenly aware that all was not well.

'What is it, love?' he asked gently. 'Is something wrong?'

'It looks as if you have conjunctivitis in both eyes.'

'I see.' They both knew that what could be a simple inflammation with a simple remedy in normally healthy eyes could, in damaged eyes, be disastrous. Corneal ulceration, diminished sight—to Emma at that moment the possibilities of stupendous consequence were overwhelming.

She phoned Hector and he came at once. He spoke to Sir Hugh on the telephone, and then handed over to James.

'Emma, my dear, Hugh wants to admit me tomorrow to his clinic. Feel like driving me down to Edinburgh?' James sounded as if he were suggesting that they go on a picnic.

'Why not? Make a nice day out,' she replied. They smiled at each other with love and understanding.

If their journey of held-back emotions was a nightmare, neither admitted it. They did not discuss the reason for going to Edinburgh. As James said, it was the first opportunity they'd had for some time to be alone together without interruption. He was wearing his dark glasses, so Emma constantly reported landmarks and places of interest.

At the clinic, James was installed in a luxurious room overlooking a gracious Italian-style garden.

Sir Hugh said, 'I'm taking Miss Seymour away with me, James. Stella's looking forward to her company. We're going to put you up, my dear, if that's all right with you.' Seeing the look on Emma's face, he added, 'I want this boy to get some rest—he'll have a hard day tomorrow with tests and examinations. Dr Reid's coming over to check out his general condition.' He turned to James. 'It's possible that this fatigue thing is having an effect on your eyes. Toby Reid will give an opinion on that.' To both of them he said, 'I'll give you five minutes for your goodbyes. I'll wait for you in the car park.' He gave Emma's arm a reassuring squeeze.

'How did he know about us?' Emma whispered when they were alone.

'He's a perceptive old bird; we must have been giving off vibes.'

James took her into his arms then and kissed her with a mixture of passion and tenderness. 'Come and see me in the morning, my darling, before they get going on me, will you?'

'Nothing and no one will stop me, sweetheart.'

She'd spent a miserable night, though the Robertsons had been marvellous hosts, wining and dining her in their gracious Georgian house in a square of equally elegant houses. They had done all that they could to make her feel at home. She had longed for bed, yet when the time had come for her to decently retire she couldn't sleep. Her thoughts had winged their way across the city to where James lay waiting to know his fate the following day.

She had visited him that morning, told him how much she loved him and that she would be thinking of him all day.

'I'll do some sightseeing,' she said. 'You're always boasting about your beautiful city.'

'You do that, love, and make sure that you go up the Scott Monument. The view's worth it.'

'I'll leave it till last, in the afternoon, then come back here to hear all the news.'

They could neither of them bring themselves to

consider in detail what might be the outcome of the investigations.

She had left then, and wandered about the city, visiting this famous museum and that famous castle, in numb, dumb misery. She went into a dim, ancient church and knelt in the Lady Chapel to pray for James, and for herself too. Whatever the outcome of today's examination, whatever the prognosis, she must not make a mistake. For both their sakes, she must make the right decision.

Over the last few days James had reiterated his feelings for her. 'I want to marry you,' he'd said. But some primitive, natural reserve had made Emma cautious. Their lifestyles were so different, to start with.

'What do you mean, darling?' he'd asked. 'You hit it off marvellously with Philippa and Angus, and Hector and his sister Maggie think that you're the best thing to hit the island since sliced bread and peanut butter!'

Emma had tried to explain. There was Nesta and her connections with exotic people who normally only appeared in the upmarket Sunday papers.

'How,' she had asked, 'do I fit in with them?'

'No better than I do,' James had replied. 'Nesta leads a life of her own.'

'But what did she mean that day when Bess was taken ill and she said that it was for her and Jamie that she had to go to Rome? It sounded very mysterious and strange.'

'She'd got mixed up with some characters who were pressing her for money that she'd lost at the gaming tables. The man she was so anxious to meet was her lover, who wanted to marry her. He'd promised to settle her debts if she met him and his father in Rome on a certain day.'

'Well,' Emma had replied, 'that makes some sense, I suppose. But how could she say that the children would benefit?'

'They apparently like Count Palestrini, and would be happy to accept him as their mother's next husband.'

'So what happened?'

'I rang the count and had a word with him. He sounds a nice enough chap. Of course, he understood that she couldn't get away to meet him at that time, with Bess ill. Only Nesta could think that he'd walk out on her if she didn't turn up. He was also quite ready to settle her debts, and, to his credit, didn't know that she has ample funds to meet such a contingency. For some reason she was reluctant to approach me about it.'

'Why should she approach you?'

'Because her husband, my best friend, appointed me a trustee to his estate, gave me control of her affairs until she made a satisfactory marriage. Not an enviable situation, and one, now, that I hope to be free of when she marries.'

'Well, that just points out what I was saying about our different ways of life. You have friends who have so much money that they need to have trust funds set up, while I'm lucky to put away enough in the building society for an occasional holiday!'

'And I, my love, have just told you that Nesta and her set are on a different plane—apart from the fact that I'm asking you to marry me and not anyone else! I assure you that my family, and those whom I consider my closest friends, think as I do: you're the tops! I just hope that you'll say yes, my darling, and put me out of my misery.'

They had been walking along the shore with a calm sea and bright warm sunshine enhancing the bay. Even then, Emma had been concerned about James. At that point he hadn't complained about his eyes, or shown signs of strain, but she, attuned to the least deviation in his health, had felt uneasy.

'Are you all right?' she'd asked when he'd stopped to look out across the water.

He'd laughed. 'I'm fine, just praying that you'll give me the right answer soon.'

She had gone to bed early that night, pleading a headache and a hangover from the events of the storm. In truth, she had wanted to avoid being alone with James after the children and Mrs Mac had retired for the night. There was no doubt in her mind or heart that she loved him, and would do forever, but she still had reservations about marrying into the MacDonald clan.

She moved round the little embrasured platform of the monument. It had been full when she'd first arrived; now there was only a middle-aged couple sharing the small space with her.

Emma looked at her watch. It was still too early to return to the clinic. No way could she bring herself to arrive back there before James had finished his tests and examinations. She couldn't sit in the consultants' rest-room, flicking through medical magazines, waiting for him to open the door and show, in his beloved face, that their worst fears had been confirmed. Much better wait and see him in the company of Sir Hugh in his consulting-room.

She stepped to the edge of the platform and gripped the balustrade, peering out into the distance as if she might find answers there.

'Are you all right, lass?' asked the middle-aged man. 'Afraid of heights?'

Emma turned and looked at him with eyes blurred with unshed tears. She shook her head.

'I'm fine, thanks, just fine.'

Neither the man nor his companion, presumably his wife, seemed convinced.

'You shouldn't stay up too long, dear,' said the woman, looking anxious. 'It's getting quite chilly, now the breeze has got up.'

Suddenly Emma realised that they were concerned about her, afraid that she might be going to do something foolish. She gave them a tremulous smile. 'I'm OK, really I am. I've just got some time to kill before going to meet a friend.' She stepped back from the balustrade. 'It's nice of you to bother.'

'It's nae bother,' said the man. 'We've a lassie of about your age—she's a nurse at the infirmary.' He sounded very proud.

'I'm a nurse,' said Emma. The couple made pleased, complimentary remarks, and she continued in an unusual rush of confidence, pleased to have a sympathetic audience, 'I'm waiting for news of a patient of mine, who's recovering from a severe illness.'

The couple exchanged knowing smiles.

'Special, is he, lass?' they asked. 'More than just a patient?'

'Yes,' said Emma, 'he is special—very special.'

'Ah!' they murmured in unison. 'Good luck to you, then. Take care, now.'

'I will—oh, I will.'

Now she knew exactly what she was going to do. Her conversation with the couple, proud of their nursing daughter, and understanding her concern for her patient, had put everything in perspective.

She would accept James's offer of marriage, whatever the outcome of his tests. If he was going to regain his full sight and ability to practise as an international plastic surgeon, so be it. Somehow she would adapt to his jet-setting lifestyle, become a perfect hostess, dress to suit the part and learn the shorthand of high society.

If, on the other hand, the fates were against him and he had to settle for a less significant role in the medical world, she would be the perfect wife and helpmate. She would risk his possible rejection of her at a later date should his masculine pride, ultimately, make him feel inadequate. What would that matter as long as she was there at the beginning to help him come to terms with his new situation?

She became aware of the fact that the sun had gone in, leaving the skies grey and the gentle breeze blowing up into a cold wind. The platform was empty. Briefly panic threatened to overwhelm her at the thought of being shut in for the night. It wasn't very late, but she hadn't seen any notices about closing time; perhaps they closed early? No, of course nothing like that had happened. The staff would have made sure that no one was on the monument. It must simply be that the weather had kept more visitors away.

Carefully she began to descend the narrow, twisting staircase. She was not afraid of heights, but negotiating the stairs in semi-gloom was quite an ordeal. Coming up had been bad enough, but then there had been dozens of people before her and after her. Also there had been people coming down from the platform. Almost everyone had been good-tempered and cheerful, apologising for bumping into each other, flattening themselves against the wall to give the maximum space to people going in the other direction.

Now the staircase was empty but for herself. She

stood hard against the wall, breathing heavily at first, and then reminding herself to control her respirations, inhaling and exhaling slowly and deliberately. It worked. She felt less claustrophobic, more in command of herself and her ultimate destination—the ground, terra firma.

There were sounds of someone coming up the staircase—slow, deliberate footsteps accompanied by a tapping sound that at first she couldn't identify. Then she realised what it was: a stick, being rhythmically tapped against stone. The rhythmic tapping that someone dependent on the sound might use; the rhythm of a blind man tapping his way up the stairs.

They met a few steps down from the platform.

'I knew you'd still be here,' said James, putting out a hand and unerringly finding hers, in spite of his protective dark glasses. 'Come, let's go to the top and look out over my beloved Edinburgh.' He grasped her hand, and she had no opportunity, even had she sought it, to do other than he suggested. She turned, and together they made their way to the top of the monument.

She said breathlessly, 'James, tell me what happened. The tests. . .'

He pulled her close to him and leaned against the rough wall. 'Dear heart,' he said, and in these surroundings it didn't seem over-sentimental, 'I love you. Will you marry me?'

Without hesitation Emma replied briskly, impatiently, 'Yes, of course I will, but James—please, darling, what about the tests?'

James kissed her. Not a very romantic or sexy kiss; in fact, it was rather matter-of-fact. 'Will my answer make any difference?'

'Of course not,' she said firmly, grateful that she had resolved to marry him whatever happened.

'Good,' he said, and continued as if he were retelling some rather dull news, 'because my eyes are going to be OK. I have an acute but mild conjunctivitis, which should heal in a few days. According to Hugh, I need you to complete my recovery.'

Emma, secure in his arms and the knowledge that she had agreed to become his wife, asked in a wondering voice, 'Me? What do you mean, me?'

'Hugh, treacherously backed up by Toby, seems to have reached the conclusion that to complete my cure in a month or so's time I need a perfect nurse, a perfect secretary and a perfect wife.' He grinned down at her. 'It seemed sensible and economic to suggest that you might fit the bill. What do you think, love?'

She paused, then said with loving conviction, 'I think it's a good prognosis and that we should abide by the recommended treatment.' She was half laughing, half crying with relief.

'Thank God for that,' said James, crushing her to his chest in a savage embrace. 'Do you know, love, there have been occasions over the last few days when I thought that you might turn me down if my eyes were going to be all right. All that nonsense about lifestyles and so on. I sometimes thought that my only chance of marrying you was to remain a dependent invalid.'

Emma, pushing away from him slightly in order to take a deep breath, said in a voice barely above a whisper, 'Oh, James, how could I, when I love you so much? I've only ever wanted what was best for you.'

'Well, you're best for me, my darling, don't ever doubt that.'

'Oh, I won't,' she said. 'I won't.'

# — *MEDICAL* ❤ *ROMANCE* —

The books for enjoyment this month are:

**DEMPSEY'S DILEMMA** Christine Adams
**WIND OF CHANGE** Clare Lavenham
**DOCTOR ON SKYE** Margaret O'Neill
**CROSSROADS OF THE HEART** Judith Worthy

❤ ❤ ❤ ❤ ❤

### Treats in store!

Watch next month for the following absorbing stories:

**SAVING DR GREGORY** Caroline Anderson
**FOR LOVE'S SAKE ONLY** Margaret Barker
**THE WRONG DIAGNOSIS** Drusilla Douglas
**ENCOUNTER WITH A SURGEON** Janet Ferguson

Available from Boots, Martins, John Menzies, W.H. Smith, most supermarkets and other paperback stockists.

Also available from Mills & Boon Reader Service, P.O. Box 236, Thornton Road, Croydon, Surrey CR9 3RU.

Readers in South Africa - write to:
Book Services International Ltd, P.O. Box 41654, Craighall, Transvaal 2024.